SUZANNE

MICHAEL BETCHERMAN

FOR CLAUDETTE AND LAURA

TUESDAY JUNE 27

Subject: Good news
From: Suzanne Braun
To: Lisa Braun

Dear Lisa,

Finally, a ray of sunshine in what has been an extraordinarily bleak year.

My dear brother-in-law has invited me to spend the summer at Inglewood, the family cottage north of Toronto. If you are puzzled by my enthusiasm, that is probably because you picture me swatting mosquitoes in the wilderness, far removed from the companionship of society. Nothing could be further from the truth. Douglas and Catherine own a place on Lake Joseph, the epicenter of establishment cottage country, and over the course of the summer I expect to meet an array of potential suitors.

The invitation could not have come at a more opportune time. Since we last spoke, I have received the final accounting from Michael's estate and my circumstances are even more dire than I had thought. In the past few years my late husband made a number of spectacularly unsuccessful investments that, combined with fourteen months of around-the-clock nursing care, have completely eroded our savings. There is nothing left except the house, and it is heavily mortgaged. Even Jennifer's college fund is gone.

My unfortunate involvement with Henry has resulted in my complete and utter exclusion from society. I am universally scorned as an opportunist who tried to take advantage of a vulnerable old man. What was I supposed to do? Meekly accept a pre-nuptial agreement that not only required me to waive my legal right to a share of his estate, but also gave him the prerogative to dismiss me at will, with a pitiful severance package? This from a man as rich as Croesus. If the situation weren't so grave, it would be humorous.

By welcoming me into the bosom of his family, my well-respected brother-in-law is announcing to one and all that my term in purgatory has officially ended. I am now free to direct my energies towards providing for my future. At the risk of sounding like a character in a Jane Austen novel, I am determined to return to Toronto at summer's end with a suitable fiancé in tow.

Jennifer will not be accompanying me to Inglewood. Relations between us were very difficult during Michael's illness - she missed no opportunity to inform me that she wished I were the one who was dying - and they have not improved since his passing. Since her expulsion from school, I have lost all semblance of control over her. She stays out until all hours of the night in the company of a variety of bizarre creatures who have apparently chosen to dedicate their lives to supporting the body piercing industry.

When I suggested that time together at the cottage would give us a chance to reconnect, she advised me that she would prefer to have her fingernails pulled off one by one rather than spend the summer in my company. Instead, she announced with an insolence I was incapable of ignoring, she would stay in the city by herself. This, I asserted, would only happen "over my dead body," a condition to which she readily agreed. The frank and candid exchange which followed convinced me to send her to camp for the summer - an all girls' camp where her hormones will have less room to rage.

Although it underscores my failure as a mother, a separation is for the best. Adolescence is proving to be a challenge that Jennifer is not capable of meeting, and I cannot imagine finding a man sweet-tempered enough to willingly expose himself to the havoc she will doubtless wreak as she blunders her way through it.

Love to you and Eduardo,

Suzanne

From: Lisa
To: Suzanne

Dearest Suzanne,

I am sorry to hear that your situation is so precarious. I have no words of sisterly advice to offer you - when it comes to attracting members of the opposite sex, you do not need my counsel.

It is understandable that you are preoccupied with finding a life partner who will provide for your earthly needs, but I pray you will be as lucky as I in finding one who will satisfy your emotional and spiritual needs as well.

Eduardo is away at the moment. My Schatzie is determined to bring the circus to Mar del Plata and is meeting with a representative of Barnum & Bailey in Buenos Aires. It will, like all his other schemes, come to nothing, but it makes him happy, and when he is happy, so am I.

Hotel business leaves me no time to mourn his absence. Although it is off-season, the weakness of the peso has ensured a steady flow of guests to Casa Blanca.

I am sorry to hear that your relationship with Jennifer continues to be the cause of so much pain but as Tanta Regina was fond of saying, "there's no use crying over spilled schnapps." All you can do is keep the door open and hope that one day Jennifer will walk through it.

Love,

Lisa

WEDNESDAY, JUNE 28

Subject: Inglewood
From: Suzanne
To: Douglas Wilkinson

Dear Douglas,

I am writing to thank you for inviting Jennifer and me to Inglewood for the summer. It is an extraordinarily generous gesture on your part and I want you to know that I will do everything in my power to ensure that Catherine and I put the past behind us. I know you and Michael both wished that our families had been closer and I deeply regret any role I may have played in keeping us apart.

Your brother's death has underlined the senselessness of holding on to ancient hurts. Our time on earth is too short to indulge in such childish behavior and I intend to honor my husband by becoming a sister-in-law to you and Catherine, and an aunt to Tony and Cleo, in spirit as well as in name.

Unfortunately Jennifer will not be joining us. As much as a separation goes against my maternal instincts, I have decided to send her to camp for the summer. As you can imagine, this has been an extremely difficult time for her and I am hopeful that a carefree summer in the company of other teenagers will restore her spirits.

My warmest regards to you and Catherine,

Suzanne

Subject: Visit to Inglewood
From: Catherine Rogers
To: Suzanne

Dear Suzanne,

I was delighted to hear from Douglas that you will be able to join us at Inglewood although I was disappointed to learn that we won't have the pleasure of Jennifer's company. I understand that she has been difficult to deal with since Michael's death – I have not been able to stop thinking about how humiliated you must have felt when she was expelled from Branksome – but even in my wildest imagination I cannot conceive of a situation becoming so untenable that a mother would feel compelled to send her child away so soon after losing her father.

Douglas told me of your desire to turn a new page in our relationship. I very much appreciate the gesture and want you to know that I embrace it in the same spirit in which it was given. I know that someone in my shoes cannot possibly know what it is like to have to start all over again. It must be a very frightening prospect and I hope you will find refuge, however temporary, here at Inglewood.

I look forward to seeing you on Saturday.

best,

Catharine

From: Suzanne
To: Catherine

Dear Catherine,

Thank you so much for inviting me to Inglewood. Everyone I know who has been there describes it in glowing terms and after hearing about it for the past eighteen years, I am eager to finally see it for myself.

I am touched by your concern for Jennifer but please rest assured that she is well. It has been several months since Michael's passing and the worst of the grieving is behind her. Although I will miss her dearly, camp is unquestionably the best place for her to be. As much as I am looking forward to spending the entire summer in your company at Inglewood, I know that if Jennifer were to do the same, she would soon descend into the depths of despair.

I appreciate your kind words of support. As you point out, it has indeed been a challenging year but it is only through struggle that we grow. If I have learned anything, it is that as much as we like to think that we know who we are, we are only one disaster away from finding out the truth about ourselves.

I look forward to seeing you on Saturday. I expect to arrive mid-afternoon.

best,

Suzanne

Subject: Suzanne
From: Catherine
To: Jean Rogers

Dear Mummy,

Douglas absolutely refuses to rescind his invitation to Suzanne. We had a huge fight about it. He as much as accused me of being responsible for his estrangement from his brother. Perhaps I was wrong to speak out so openly against the marriage but surely her escapade with Henry proves I was right about the little golddigger all along.

I know Douglas feels terribly guilty about the rift with Michael and that this is his way of making amends, so if I want to preserve the peace at home I suppose I'll have to go along. The one silver lining is that Suzanne is shipping her daughter off to camp for the summer. I feel sorry for the poor girl - what kind of mother would abandon her daughter so soon after her father's death? - but I'm relieved that I won't have to deal with her. From all accounts she has inherited her mother's sense of morality. Maggie told me that the reason she was expelled from Branksome was because she tried to recruit some of her classmates to pose for a pornographic website. Not an influence I would care to have Tony and Cleo exposed to.

Mark called tonight from Tokyo. He ran into some last-minute problems with Jeff but they finally closed the deal today. I think he's happy to be leaving Japan for good. He's not going to forget Keiko overnight - they were together a long time - but it'll be a lot easier once he puts 6,000 miles between them. He's going to London tomorrow to spend a few days with Patrick before he comes to Inglewood.

On the drive up, I showed Cleo a monster house and asked her if she would like to live there. She said no, I don't want to live with monsters. Isn't that the cutest thing you ever heard?

Love to you and Daddy. Hope you're enjoying the cruise. Tony and I have already started working on his geography project for next year so don't forget to send us stamps from your various ports of call.

Love,

Catherine

From: Jean
To: Catherine

Darling,

Has Douglas taken leave of his senses? I can understand that he feels obliged to make a gesture towards Suzanne, but to indulge himself by inviting her for the entire summer verges on the sinful.

The timing simply couldn't be worse. Suzanne is obviously hunting for a new husband and I shudder to think what will happen if she gets it in her mind to pursue your brother. Mark is in a very vulnerable state right now. He's like me, sensitive to a fault - you're so lucky you inherited your father's thick skin - and that makes him easy prey for a pretty face and a sympathetic ear. I won't pretend to be sorry that things have ended with Keiko. I've known from the start that things weren't going to work out - the Japanese like to stick to their own as much as we do - but I hope he isn't about to jump from the frying pan into the fire.

This is the first we've heard about Mark having problems with the sale of the business. Don't tell Mark, but Daddy and I are both very disappointed that we had to find out from you.

Cleo's comment about the monster house is simply adorable. I'm going to send it in to Reader's Digest.

Love to everybody,

Mummy

THURSDAY, JUNE 29

Subject: Leaving Japan
From: Mark Rogers
To: Catherine

Hey,

I'm waiting for the cab to take me to the airport. It's a dreary day here in Tokyo which pretty much matches my mood. I spent the last couple of days saying my goodbyes. It was totally depressing, everywhere I turned I was reminded of all the good times Keiko and I had. I called her up today to say goodbye but of course I just ended up getting mad at her. Easier than being mad at myself, I guess. The truth is I've known for a long time that when push came to shove, she wouldn't go against her family's wishes and marry a gaijin, let alone have kids with him. She denies it of course, but my guess is that she'll be married to a Japanese guy and pregnant within the year.

I'm not as bitter as I sound. Okay, maybe I am, but I don't have any regrets about forcing the issue. I know I want a family and it was never going to happen with Keiko. It's just too bad it took me 14 years to figure it out.

Patrick and I are going hiking in the Lake District for a few days, so I probably won't get to Inglewood until the end of next week. I hope you and Suzanne will have sorted things out by then. Yes, Douglas shouldn't have invited her without asking you first, but she's not going to eat your young so as long as she's going to be there, you might as well make the best of it. Weren't you listening in Sunday school when they told us to turn the other cheek?

Look forward to seeing everybody. I'll be in touch when I've firmed up my plans.

sayonara

Mark

From: Catherine
To: Mark

I'd be happy to turn the other cheek if I didn't know Suzanne would slap that one too.

Mummy's peeved she that she had to find out about your problems with Jeff from me. Do us both a favor and drop her a line.

Catherine

Subject: Hi
From: Mark
To: Jean

Hi Mom. Sorry I haven't been much of a correspondent lately but the last couple of weeks have been very hectic. Jeff and I had some issues with the payout terms and at one point it looked like the deal was going to fall apart. I suppose I could have forced the issue but that would have meant staying in Tokyo until we resolved things. There was a lot of money involved, but when push came to shove I decided it was more important to get on with my life.

Please don't worry about me. I'm fine. What happened with Keiko is ancient history as far as I'm concerned. Nothing can take away the fact that we had 14 wonderful years together. That's a lot more than most couples have and I wouldn't trade away a single day, even if things didn't turn out the way I hoped.

Hope you and dad are enjoying the cruise. Look forward to seeing you at Inglewood when you get back.

Mark

MONDAY, JULY 3

Subject: the wicked witch of the west
From: Catherine
To: Maggie Stern

Hi Mags,

Well, the she-devil arrived Saturday afternoon, laden with six Louis Vuitton suitcases and the touching declaration that her "fondest desire" was that we put the past behind us. She's been on her best behavior: gracious towards me, deferential towards Douglas, and doting towards the children. That sound you hear is me retching.

My foolish husband has been completely taken in. He is convinced that Suzanne is sincere about wanting to turn over a new leaf. When I muttered something about a wolf in designer clothing, he accused me of being mean-spirited and suggested that I was jealous of Suzanne because I had been 'going with' Michael when he met her. Have you ever heard anything more absurd? A handful of unmemorable dates hardly qualifies as 'going with' someone. If anyone is jealous, it's Douglas. Why else would he dredge this up after all these years?

Michael's the one he should be angry at. I don't like to speak poorly about the dead, but if he'd had the courage to stand up to Suzanne, none of this would ever have happened. He and

Douglas were as close to each other growing up as Mark and I were. Can you imagine either of us letting anyone get between us like she did with them? Then again, perhaps I'm being too hard on Michael. The woman is a remarkably nasty piece of business. It's only taken her a day to set Douglas and I against each other. She had years to work on Michael.

Have you decided if you're going to enroll Emma at TFS? I know Cleo will be thrilled if the two of them are in the same class. Don't worry about Emma's French not being up to speed. If it's any reassurance, none of the other kids are as fluent as Cleo. Having Francoise as a nanny has given her a huge leg up, although if I say so myself, Cleo does have a natural ear for languages. We started in on Spanish last week and she can already count to a hundred. Anyway, if you do go ahead, we can always schedule some French only play-dates when Francoise gets back from Brittany.

love to David and the kids,

Catherine

From: Maggie
To: Catherine

Hi Cat,

You know how much I love Douglas, but it was very disloyal of him to invite Suzanne to Inglewood without clearing it with you first. And that crack about you being jealous was way out of line. The point is that she went after Michael while you were still seeing him. Whether or not you were interested in him, and of course you weren't, is completely irrelevant. You don't do that to a friend. But then, she never was interested in being our friend, was she? We were just her ticket to the right side of the tracks. I wonder if it has ever crossed her mind that if we hadn't befriended her, she would never have met Michael in the first place. Remember that god awful yellow jump suit she was wearing the first day of class?

I happened to see her at Holt's a couple of days ago. Truly depressing. The woman doesn't age. If there is a God, she really does move in mysterious ways. If I was in charge, I wouldn't have wasted the boils on the Egyptians, I'd have saved them for her. She was her usual phony self, declared herself 'absolutely thrilled' to see me. yadda yadda yadda. I guess she lost my number when it came time to put her house up for sale. By the way, she dropped the price a second time even though her agent suggested she take it off the market until things pick up. Michael must have left her in worse shape than we thought.

I have to admit she's got nerve. Her parting words were 'I hope we'll get a chance to see you at Inglewood," as if her name was on title. Why don't you put her up in the boathouse? Maybe the raccoons will persuade her she's not welcome.

We decided to send Emma to TFS. Yay! You were so right that we shouldn't worry about her French. The principal said that at this age it makes absolutely no difference how much French kids speak, and that in a few months Emma would be speaking as well as any of the other kids.

When does Françoise return? I'm so envious that you're keeping her on even though Cleo will be at school all day. David would never indulge me like that.

xoxo
Maggie

Marjorie Stern
Oak Tree Realty
Everything Maggie touches turns to SOLD!!!

From: Suzanne
To: Lisa

Dear Lisa,

I arrived at Inglewood Saturday after dropping Jennifer off at camp. Any doubts I had about the wisdom of placing her there were dispelled two minutes after we arrived when, in full view of everyone, she loudly announced that I could leave and then brusquely rebuffed my attempt to hug her goodbye. If she didn't bear such an eerie resemblance to me, I would be convinced that she had been switched at birth.

Douglas and the children were out when I arrived, leaving Catherine free to provide a welcome - a slab of orange cheddar, some stale crackers and the remains of an open bottle of wine - that clearly defined the rules of engagement. I am the poor relative with nowhere else to go; she is the benevolent lady of the manor, duty bound to take me in.

What happened next convinced me that I am faced with an adversary who will stop at nothing to get rid of me. Once we exchanged pleasantries, she asked if I would like to see some pictures of the children. Before I could tell her that I would rather be jabbed in the eye with a hot needle, she advanced towards me with a hideous grin and a daunting stack of photo albums. At first I thought she intended to crush me to death with them but that would have left marks. It was only by the end of the first album, when baby Tony had rolled over onto his side for the third time in his life, that her fiendish plan became clear. She intends to bore me to death.

Catherine is a charter member of that tribe of dull women who live vicariously through their children, obsessively immersing themselves in every detail of their lives and tirelessly singing their praises. If her children are even one-tenth as talented as she claims, before the summer is out Tony will be offered a Rhodes Scholarship and Cleo's artwork will be removed from the fridge and installed at the Whitney.

After half an hour I could feel the life force draining out of me when Douglas came to the rescue. He seemed genuinely pleased to see me. At the risk of sounding immodest, I think he is happy to have me here on aesthetic grounds alone. Catherine's best years - a relative term - are long past. If they are still having conjugal relations, it is only because he is burdened with an extraordinarily strong sense of duty.

The children however, are a pleasant surprise. They are neither as dull and unimaginative as their gene pool would suggest, nor as spoiled and self-centered as their upbringing would lead one to predict. Although they are as different as night and day -

Tony is an introvert, happy to spend his days with his nose in a book while Cleo is outgoing and energetic - they get along beautifully with each other. Tony takes his responsibility as a big brother very seriously and Cleo absolutely idolizes him. I couldn't help wondering if Jennifer might have turned out differently had I been able to provide her with a sibling.

The cottage itself is lovely - a little run-down in that charming way which only the rich can pull off - and I am sure I shall be very comfortable here. It was built a half-century ago by Catherine's grandfather, Grandpa Jack, and it is a point of honor with her that everything remain in its original state. This year Douglas finally rebelled at his wife's reverence for tradition and installed an indoor toilet - a state-of-the-art composting toilet that converts you-know-what into black earth for his vegetable garden. (Note to self: avoid vegetables for the duration.) Within minutes of his arrival he showed off his new toy. He was so proud of it that for a moment I feared he was going to give me a personal demonstration.

Grandpa Jack's original outhouse is still standing and Catherine continues to use it when the weather cooperates. She contends that the view of the lake it provides on a moonlit night is an experience that shouldn't be missed. Not an image one is keen to linger on.

More later. An interminable evening of board games awaits. Is 'bitch' in the official Scrabble dictionary?

Love,

Suzanne

WEDNESDAY, JULY 5

Subject: Suzanne
From: Catherine
To: Jean

Dear Mummy,

I know I shouldn't let it get to me, not with my thick skin, but if things keep up the way they're going my marriage won't survive the summer.

Yesterday the Wards called up to invite us to a cocktail party. Douglas made sure that Suzanne was included. I could have killed him. We were an hour late waiting for her to get dressed. She finally emerged in a pair of shorts - short being the operative word - and a low scoop neck t-shirt that had the men salivating the moment she bounced off the boat. Earl Stewart, loaded as usual, immediately started chatting her up but the look he got from Elisa sobered him up in a hurry. After that, the others were smart enough to keep their distance.

Roger Dillon was there as well. He's throwing his annual bash this Saturday at the club. Suzanne was desperate for an invite and threw out a number of feelers, all of which Roger pointedly ignored. Not surprising, considering that he and Henry are such good friends. Most people would have got the hint but not our Suzanne. She cornered Roger when he was talking to Douglas and me and asked him outright if she could come to the party. Can you believe the gall of the woman? The poor man was caught completely off-guard. Talk about an awkward silence. He said yes, of course. What else could he do with Douglas standing right there? Tell one of his best clients that his houseguest wasn't welcome at his party?

I thought, if nothing else, that this would at least remove the blinkers from Douglas' eyes, and that he would finally see her for what she is. I even dared to think he would feel so insulted by her outrageous behavior that he would send her packing. Fat chance. He was insulted - but by Roger, not Suzanne. He said he didn't give a damn about Roger's friendship with Henry, Suzanne was our guest and if she was good enough to be invited into our home, then she was good enough to be invited to his damn party. He actually chuckled about the way Suzanne made Roger squirm. Said it served him right.

Love,

Catherine

From: Jean
To: Catherine

Darling,

Has Roger gone senile? He should have told the little tart she wasn't welcome at the party, Douglas or no Douglas. Poor you. Saturday will be hell but you will just have to grin and bear it.

I finally heard from Mark and my baby's in even worse shape than I thought. He's putting up a brave front but I can tell that Keiko has broken his heart. He was so desperate to leave his painful memories behind that he let Jeff renegotiate the buyout. Like your father says, you got to hand it to the Jews, they're great businessmen. And if you don't hand it to them, they'll take it.

I'm afraid we're headed for a real catastrophe unless we do something about Suzanne. You know how I hate to interfere but you simply must get Douglas to change his mind. Don't you think it's time to adopt a different strategy? Getting angry obviously isn't working. There are many ways to a man's heart. With some, it's a matter of appealing to their vanity. Others respond to a special kind of intimate attention. Some men cannot bear the sight of a woman in tears. You've been with the man for nearly two decades. Surely you know where his weak spots are.

Love,

Mummy

From: Catherine
To: Jean

Douglas' only weak spot is that he is as stubborn as a mule. But I'm open to suggestions.

From: Jean
To: Catherine

My only advice is to remind you that he is a man and therefore constitutionally incapable of admitting he has made a mistake. This does not mean the situation is hopeless. Fifty years of marriage have taught me that the male of the species can be persuaded to change his mind, but only if he thinks he is doing it of his own accord.

From: Suzanne
To: Lisa

Dear Lisa:

Yesterday we went to a cocktail party at a cottage across the lake. After being marooned at the cottage for three tedious days with nothing to do but listen to Catherine coo with delight every time one of her prodigies uttered a word without stuttering, the change of scene came as a welcome relief.

Unfortunately, there was not a bachelor in sight. Which is not to say that the outing was devoid of entertainment. One of the guests, an obnoxious fool who confirmed my belief that self-made men are among the least agreeable of the species, mistook my friendly conversation as a sign that I found him irresistible. Emboldened by several martinis, he took me aside and told me how much he enjoyed talking to me. Then, staring deep into my cleavage, he declared that he would love to pursue our conversation at a later date, say tomorrow afternoon at the

Village Inn. I told him this was a lovely idea and suggested we ask his wife to join us. From the look of consternation that crossed his face, I could only assume that he was suffering from an advanced case of dementia and had completely forgotten that he was married. His wife soon joined us and it was heartrending to witness the look of horror that crossed his face as his memory came flooding back.

Happily the evening was not a total loss on the social front. I have been invited to a party this Saturday at the golf club, an annual event that kicks off the summer season. A number of eligible bachelors are certain to be in attendance, and from a smattering of phrases I overheard as Catherine and her friends discussed their various attributes - "made a fortune from the IPO", "bills out at $950 an hour", "bought the penthouse apartment for $7 million, and then gutted the place" - I am hopeful I may finally meet my soul mate.

Catherine was dismayed to learn that I had been invited to the party. Indeed, I did not think the human face capable of contorting itself into a look as sour as the one that graced her face when she found out. Then again, a week in her company has caused me to question my most basic assumptions. For example, I had not thought it possible that a human being could memorize every two-letter word in the Scrabble dictionary, nor that victory in a game of Monopoly could be the source of such visceral satisfaction, but on both counts she has proven me wrong.

Love,

Suzanne

SUNDAY, JULY 9

Subject: Suzanne
From: Catherine
To: Jean

Dear Mummy,

Suzanne was on the prowl last night at the Dillon's party, dressed in full hunting regalia - a skimpy summer frock that left nothing to the imagination. You should have seen the parade of drooling men who happened to pass by our table. I swear at one point they actually formed a line. I felt like handing out numbers. It never ceases to amaze me what simpletons men are. How did we ever let them get in charge?

After culling the herd, no doubt in consultation with Dun & Bradstreet, she has set her sights on Gary McCoy. I was surprised - not that he was attracted by her tawdry charms, he is a man, after all - but that he was willing to cavort with her in public, as opposed, say, to a clandestine tryst at the Village Inn. As for Suzanne, she must be even more desperate than I imagined. I had forgotten how mind-numbingly boring Gary could be. He was so tedious that Douglas, who hasn't danced with me since the Dow was below 5,000, kept me out on the floor until it was time to go home.

The two of them spent the evening deep in conversation, and

Gary called first thing this morning to invite her out for dinner tonight. He hasn't been involved with anyone since he and Sonia divorced. I heard she took him to the cleaners and he's apparently been gun-shy ever since. Well, if he thought Sonia was trouble, he ain't seen nothing yet.

The club hired a new pastry chef from L.A. and whoever's responsible should be locked up. He made a Gateau St. Honoré so delicious that I couldn't resist going for seconds. Fortunately I was able to work it off on the dance floor.

Everybody asked about the two of you and wanted to know when you were coming up. Ed Harvey was his usual obnoxious self. He said he noticed daddy hadn't entered the club championship yet and asked if it was on account of the "thrashing" he gave him last year.

Love,

Catherine

From: Jean
To: Catherine

Darling,

Very interesting about Gary and Suzanne. I highly doubt that someone as conservative as he is would be seriously interested in Suzanne. Can you imagine him escorting her to the Brazilian ball? His father would have a conniption fit. But let's hope it will at least develop into something that will distract her for the rest of the summer. If she were to direct her "tawdry charms" towards Mark, I am not sure he would be able to put up much resistance. Tawdry is in the eye of the beholder, and I do not have to tell you that the male of the species does not behold in the same way we women do.

The cruise has been delightful. Yesterday we went into Singapore with Tom and Elaine Cunningham, a couple from Seattle we've become friendly with. Tom was in advertising and he and Daddy spent the better part of the day in the bar at Raffles swapping war stories. Elaine and I went to the National Museum. She was on the board of the Seattle Art Museum for many years and arranged for the curator to give us a private tour.

Elaine has a granddaughter the same age as Cleo. She can't stop talking about how cute she is, although judging by the pictures she's shown me, she clearly doesn't qualify as an objective witness. I was hoping to staunch the deluge by showing her the video of Cleo at Sandbanks but I couldn't find it on the Internet. How do I get to it?

Love,

Mummy

PS. Daddy says to tell Ed Harvey that he will be back in time for the club championship, and to remind him that every time a player swings the club it counts as a stroke, whether or not he actually hits the ball.

From: Catherine
To: Jean

Just go to YouTube.com and search for "Cleo at Sandbanks." If that doesn't give you bragging rights, nothing will.

From: Suzanne
To: Lisa

Dear Lisa,

I met a wonderful man at the party last night. His name is Gary McCoy and he is as attractive and charming as one would expect from a man who is a senior partner in a prestigious law firm, and the heir – the sole heir - of one of the country's most successful real estate developers.

Gary captivated me with his sparkling wit the moment he came to our table and critiqued the table wine with a detailed description so droll that it had my brother-in-law begging for mercy. I believe his exact words were "would someone please shoot me and put me out of my misery."

Douglas was sensitive enough to give Gary and I time to get to know each other and when Catherine returned from her third trip to the dessert table, he took her out on the dance floor. After a truly frightening moment when I mistook her frenzied dancing style for an epileptic fit, I was able to give Gary my full attention.

Although his interest in me seemed genuine, I was naturally wary of his motives. If he shared the prevailing opinion that I had treated Henry poorly, his intentions could not possibly be honorable. But Gary immediately set my mind to rest. He told me that his law firm represented Henry and, unlike the mindless herd that had been so quick to judge me, he was familiar with the details of our negotiations. In his opinion, he said, I was guilty only of separating matters of business from affairs of the heart, an attitude for which he had the highest respect.

We then moved on to more agreeable topics and I soon observed that he is not one of those men with whom having a conversation is akin to pulling teeth. The breadth of his knowledge of employment law is nothing short of astounding, as is his willingness to share it, and although I might quibble with his opinion that unions should be outlawed and the minimum wage abolished, he said nothing to diminish the favorable impression I had of him. Indeed, he carries himself with such presence that I did not realize he was six inches shorter than me until our first dance together.

He has invited me to dinner tonight. My search for true love may be over.

Love,

Suzanne

MONDAY, JULY 10

Subject: Gary M
From: Maggie
To: Catherine

Hi Cat,

What's this I hear about Suzanne and Gary McCoy? Isobel told me the two were thick as thieves at Roger's party. Is this just a one-night stand, or is it something we're going to be able to sink our teeth into?

Talk soon,

Marjorie Stern
Oak Tree Realty
Everything Maggie touches turns to SOLD!!!

From: Catherine
To: Maggie

Hi Mags,

Too early to say where this is going. It's no mystery how Suzanne feels. This is definitely love at first sight - of Gary's inheritance. As for Gary, it's either temporary insanity, a mid-life crisis, or both. He's taking her to Stadtlander's tonight, overkill in my opinion if all he's after is a roll in the hay. But whatever his intentions, here's hoping he keeps Suzanne away from Inglewood as much as possible.

The woman has made my life an absolute hell. I'll spare you the gory details. Suffice to say that I'm doing my best to stay out of her way. It means I never get to use the mirror but that's a small price to pay. The woman has taken vanity to new heights. I swear she puts on makeup to go to the bathroom. And someone must have told her there's a bylaw against wearing the same outfit twice.

Meanwhile my mother's driving me crazy worrying about Mark. She's convinced that he is so heartbroken that he's going to sink into the depths of despair and will either end up running back to Keiko or even worse, succumb to Suzanne's so-called charms. She's always been so protective of him. If he so much as scraped his knee, she'd be dialling 911. It's amazing he didn't end up gay. With me, unless a bone broke the skin, it was a band-aid and a pat on the head. I know it's because he was a preemie but you'd think she'd be over it by now. The man is 42 years old after all.

My one consolation has been trouncing Suzanne at Scrabble. For some reason she thought her degree in 19th century English literature would give her an edge and although she pretends not to care, it kills her to lose to someone who freely admits to being bored by Pride and Prejudice. If she tells me one more time how "clever" - read shallow - I am, I think I'll scream.

Tonight - to avoid another loss, no doubt - she offered to read Cleo her bedtime story. I suggested a bible story would be appropriate, the one where the serpent arrives in the Garden of Eden.

love,

Catherine

Subject: Dinner with My Prince
From: Suzanne
To: Lisa

Dear Lisa,

Gary and I had a lovely dinner tonight at a farmhouse restaurant run by one of the country's most famous chefs. One normally has to wait months to get a reservation but Gary's firm represents the restaurant and he was able to get us a table on one day's notice.

It was the best meal I have ever had, an eight-course extravaganza that no conversation could possibly measure up to, although Gary cannot be faulted for a lack of effort. As I sampled a sublime duck gizzard confit, he regaled me with an account of his latest case, a fascinating story about a collective agreement in the food services industry that did not come to its stirring conclusion until I had digested my main course, a filet of perch pan-fried in lemon-Pernod butter.

For dessert I had an exquisite maple mousse covered by a blanket of chocolate-flecked Lübeck marzipan while Gary established beyond a reasonable doubt that his ex-wife Sonia is a malicious bitch.

Although they had initially agreed to joint custody of their two boys as part of their divorce, Sonia is now threatening to go to court to gain sole custody. Gary fears that because they are so young Sonia may be successful, particularly since his workload in the past few months has been so heavy that he has rarely been home. He was most distraught. He is utterly devoted to the boys and spent the rest of the evening whimpering at the prospect of losing them. He was so forthcoming that I will never again complain that men do not share their feelings.

His anguish was heartfelt and my sympathy for his plight was undiminished by the fact that fate has blessed him to be the sole heir to a considerable fortune. I cannot overstate the tender feelings I felt towards him when he walked me to the door of Inglewood and stood on his tiptoes to give me a goodnight kiss.

Tomorrow he is taking me on an outing to "sample the cultural attractions of Muskoka." I am positively giddy with excitement.

love,

Suzanne

WEDNESDAY, JULY 12

From: Suzanne
To: Lisa

Dear Lisa,

Gary drove back to the city tonight to take care of pressing business but I have the memory of our day together to sustain me until his return.

The darling man escorted me on a comprehensive tour of every art gallery within a fifty-mile radius of Inglewood. The local artists are so productive that I do not think there is a tree in Muskoka that has escaped their notice, and Gary was exceedingly generous about sharing his detailed knowledge of their work.

It was one of those summer days that seems to last forever.

In the course of our journey we encountered a number of Gary's fellow cottagers and the affection he showered on me in the face of their coldness towards me — is there anyone in the entire world who does not know about Henry and me? - convinced me that he was indifferent to their petty judgments.

My growing feeling that I had good reason to be optimistic about our future was cemented at the end of the day when the dear man inquired about my intentions. He told me that at this stage in his life he was looking for a serious relationship and that if I were only interested in a summer romance it would be best for us to part company here and now. I hastened to assure him that the thought of the two of us having a casual fling could not be further from my mind. I could have gone on to say that I was as likely to entertain the notion of spending a month in a leper colony, but there seemed no need to belabor the point.

My hopes that we might end the day by deepening our relationship were dashed when he announced that he had a business meeting early in the morning and that he would have to drive straight back to Toronto. I suggested we stop at his place for a nightcap but he demurred. Apparently the poor man cannot function without eight hours of sleep. He has invited me to spend the weekend at his cottage, by which time I pray he will be more rested.

Love,

Suzanne

Subject: Mark
From: Catherine
To: Jean

Dear Mummy,

I just spoke to Mark. He's flying to Toronto on Sunday and will come straight up to Inglewood. We had a long chat and trust me, you don't have to worry that your sensitive son will spend the summer pining away for Keiko. He's upset, of course — they were together for a long time - but what really bothers him is the thought that he wasted all those years with her when he could have been raising a family of his own.

I wouldn't worry about him falling for Suzanne either. He's not looking for a wife so much as a broodmare. My guess is that he'll fall for the first fertile woman who canters into sight. That in itself should lay your fears about Suzanne to rest. She may have a few childbearing years left in her but the last thing she wants is another child. The woman does not have a maternal bone in her body. The other day I asked her how Jennifer was doing and I swear it took her a few seconds to figure out who I was talking about.

In any event, her priorities lie elsewhere. Her plan to ensnare Gary is underway and it appears to be moving ahead nicely. He took her to Eigensinn Farm last night, and today they spent the entire day together. He just dropped her off on his way back to the city and from the look of enchantment on his face and the one of satisfaction on hers, it looks like he's swallowed whatever witch's brew she's been serving up. She's in her room cackling right now.

love,

Catherine

FRIDAY, JULY 14

Subject: Waiting for my prince
From: Suzanne
To: Lisa

Dear Lisa,

The days have been passing slowly since Gary went to town, but his nightly calls have been a great comfort. I have never met a man who so ardently believes that a relationship between a man and a woman must be between two equals. Rather than unilaterally deciding that a certain detail of his life is trivial and insignificant, he gives me the honor of making that determination for myself. Short of breaching lawyer-client privilege, which he holds sacred, there is no aspect of his work about which he is not desirous of enlightening me. Another week of this and I believe I will be able to pass the bar exams.

He is arriving shortly to take me to his cottage for the weekend, and although nothing could be more exciting than the opportunity to further my legal education, the prospect of a few days away from Catherine runs a very close second.

It is difficult to say which of her character traits is most insufferable - there is no lack of contenders for the title - but if I were pressed to choose I would point to her smug satisfaction with her life. I do not begrudge her the ease of her existence; it would be hypocritical of me to do so. What irks me is the congratulatory attitude she has about her good fortune, as if it is a reflection of her own accomplishments and not an accident of birth.

This morning we went on a tour of the lake which gave her an opportunity to give voice to one of her favorite laments: the deplorable changes that have taken place over the past twenty years, ever since the nouveau riche moved in and replaced modest cottages like Inglewood with multi-million dollar mansions. Her objections cannot possibly be on aesthetic grounds - with the way she dresses, just plop her in the cornfield and you'll never have to worry about the crows again. No, she prefers the look of her weather-beaten cottage, perched as it is on several million dollars of lakefront, because it demonstrates the blithe disregard for money that those who have always had it like to believe separates them from those who have only recently acquired it.

Her elitist attitude both offends and saddens me. It is depressing to know that in the 21st century there are those who still insist on judging a man by the circumstances of his birth. I firmly believe that it matters not whether a man has inherited his millions, or whether he has made them through the sweat of his own labor. In my mind the two are equally worthy.

Love,

Suzanne

Subject: Suzanne and Gary
From: Catherine
To: Maggie

Hi Mags,

It looks like the relationship between Gary and Suzanne is the real deal. From the size of the bouquet that arrived today, it appears that he is completely besotted. He's been in the city the past few days but he calls her every night. They talk for ages - Gary does most of the talking, surprise, surprise - and if it weren't for the glazed look in her eyes, Suzanne's girlish giggles would have you believe he has miraculously acquired a sense of humor. I don't think I have ever before seen anyone stifle a yawn and convincingly whisper "I miss you" at the same time.

Tony started sailing camp on Monday. He kicked up a storm about it at first, but once I told him those awful Henderson boys wouldn't be there, he settled down and said he'd go. I worry so much about him. The world is a cruel place for a sensitive boy like him.

How did Zach's tryout go?

Love to David and the kids,

Catherine

From: Maggie
To: Catherine

Hi Cat,

Wonders will never cease. I bumped into Helen McTeague at the club and she said she saw Suzanne and Gary walking around Port Carling hand-in-hand, staring at each other like a couple of moonstruck teenagers.

By the way, I don't know if it's true, but there's a rumor going around that Gary's father isn't well. Word is they're keeping it quiet because they don't want to spook the market.

I'm glad you talked Tony into going to sailing camp. I'm sure he'll have a great time without those bullies there to torture him. It was that damn counselor's fault, if he'd stepped in the first time they called Tony a 'momma's boy', it would never have gotten out of hand.

Zach made the rep team. We're so proud of him. The competition was ferocious and most of the kids were a lot bigger than he is but he is absolutely fearless. David and I have no idea where he got that from. Probably because of the shameful way we neglected him. Guess he had to learn how to fend for himself.

talk soon,

Marjorie Stern
Oak Tree Realty
Everything Maggie touches turns to SOLD

SATURDAY, JULY 15

Subject: back from the cottage
From: Suzanne
To: Lisa

Dear Lisa,

The best laid plans … I'm sure there's a pun that could be made here but until I can come up with one, suffice to say that the weekend with Gary didn't exactly go according to script.

It got off to a very promising start. Gary had invited his friend Stuart, a lawyer who works for his father, and his wife to spend the day with us, and he was exceedingly demonstrative with his affections towards me in front of them, giving the impression that we had already achieved an intimacy I was now certain we would attain before night's end.

My sense of anticipation grew as we lingered over a four-course dinner Gary had prepared using only locally produced ingredients. An exhaustive description of the provenance of each element of the meal naturally led to an illuminating explanation of the environmental benefits of sustainable agriculture. As he segued into a dissertation on the history of the early settlers of Muskoka, I allowed my mind to wander, and it was pleasant to imagine myself spending my summers here. I saw myself taking long solitary walks in the woods on the weekends when Gary was with me, and then, during the week when he was in town, I would be kept busy supervising the young man I will have to hire to help maintain the grounds.

It was nearly midnight when dinner finally came to a close. Stuart's wife excused herself and went up to bed. Stuart was about to follow when Gary embroiled him in a discussion about the dangers posed to society by unregulated paralegals. He was convinced that permitting laymen to defend parking tickets was the start down a slippery slope that would inevitably lead to a breakdown of the entire judicial system. Nobody who witnessed the vigor with which he defended his position – his outrage did not subside until two a.m. - could ever again claim that lawyers lack passion. That should have been my first clue that events were not likely to unfold as I had anticipated.

After Stuart went to bed, I was confident we were about to move our relationship to the next level - upstairs. I was feeling very warmly disposed towards Gary, and murmured something to that effect to him. He blushed, began clearing off the table, and did not stop until the food was put away, the dishwasher loaded, and the kitchen floor swept. Short of applying a fresh coat of paint to the walls, there was nothing left to do. That should have been my second clue.

It was nearly three a.m. when we finally retired to the bedroom. When I emerged from the washroom, Gary had fallen into a deep sleep from which he could not be roused. I needed no more clues. The conclusion that he was fearful of an intimate encounter was unavoidable.

By the time I awoke the following morning, Stuart and his wife had already left. I considered confronting Gary but decided against it. I have had enough experience with lawyers to realize that it would not matter if truth was on my side, I would lose the argument. Best, I decided, to allow Gary to dictate the pace of our relationship. After all, I had an entire weekend in which to allay his fears. Or so I thought, until he told me that his father had been rushed to hospital, and he would have to return to town.

When we arrived at Inglewood, he escorted me down to the dock to say hello to my hosts. The warmth of his goodbye elicited a forlorn look from Douglas as he contemplated the barrenness of his marriage, and an encouraging smile from Catherine whose hope that Gary will spirit me away from Inglewood is no less powerful than my own,

Love,

Suzanne

From: Lisa
To: Suzanne

Dear Suzanne,

I applaud your sensitive handling of the situation. The greater Gary's fears, the more gently he must be treated. I had much the same experience with Eduardo when we first met. He was so devoted to his mother that had I not built the casita for her on the hotel grounds, he might never have left her home. It was not always easy having her so close at hand, but it was the only way I could have my Schatzie. Although it has been three years since she passed on, he continues to seek her advice, and the casita, which he regards as a shrine to her memory, remains exactly as she left it.

Eduardo sends his love. His failure to find investors for the circus has not dimmed his optimism. Today he told me that he was going to promote a space voyage to the sun. "But it's a million degrees on the sun," I said. "Everybody will be burnt to death." My Schatzie was unfazed. "We'll go at night," he said.

I am sending along a newspaper article that may give you some insight into the forces that have shaped Gary.

Love,

Lisa

He's the Real McCoy
By Denise Skelton
Special to the Financial Times

He's the driving force behind the world's fifth largest commercial real estate development company but few people have heard of Isaac McCoy. The reclusive head of McCoy Development Corp. shuns publicity no less ferociously than Donald Trump seeks it. You won't find McCoy slicking his hair back in front of the nearest camera. Your best bet is to head out any Wednesday morning at 5 a.m. to the nondescript building in a Toronto suburb that houses the Evangelical Synod of Upper Canada. Look for the elderly man with a long white beard and a mop in his hand.

It's no exercise in media manipulation. McCoy has had Wednesday floor-mopping duty for the past 27 years, ever since he and the other elders in the ESUC broke away from their former church and established a separate congregation. McCoy explained that the rift arose when his former church attempted to finesse its way through the theory of evolution by claiming that each "day" of creation lasted an eon or two. To McCoy and his fellow travelers, this was heresy. They believe that the Holy Scriptures are divinely inspired and that everything contained in them is the literal truth. McCoy claimed to bear no animosity over the breakup, and asked that his former church not be identified as he had "no desire to embarrass the sinners in public, the Lord will deal with them in his own way."

McCoy's faith dates back to his youth, when he was stricken with polio. Showing an innate talent for deal making, he promised God that if he were healed he would devote his life to him, and contribute 20% of every dollar he ever made to the church. The Lord came through and McCoy has kept his end of the bargain ever since.

Even in 1992 when the bottom fell out of the world property market and his company was on the verge of bankruptcy, McCoy never lost his faith. In fact, he credits God for giving him the advice he needed to survive the crisis. He'd sunk most of his company's funds into a mega project in Singapore and with construction well underway his major tenants backed out. Replacements were harder to find than a rich man in the kingdom of heaven, and he was forced to hand the keys over to his creditors. The pundits were predicting ruin but God came to Isaac in a dream. "He said one sentence to me, just one," McCoy recalled. "Behold, I will give your enemy into your hand, and you shall do to him as it shall seem good to you." The quote, from 1 Samuel 24 for those of you who weren't paying attention in Sunday school, may seem cryptic but McCoy wasn't confused. He managed to persuade his creditors to let him manage the property they had just seized from him. The agreement included a buyback clause that nobody thought he'd ever be able to exercise, but three years later when the market picked up he did just that.

From that day on McCoy has taken counsel from his supreme advisor, and it's given him an edge over his less well-connected competitors. In recent days rumors that the 77 year-old McCoy is not well have been circulating on Wall Street. McCoy, who looked frail but spoke vigorously, said he'd received a clean bill of health from his doctors but, not surprisingly, offered that "the Lord will take me at a time of his own choosing." McCoy acknowledged that the market was interested in knowing who would succeed him as company CEO, but said it was premature to discuss the issue. His son Gary, a prominent lawyer in Toronto, is the logical choice but relations between he and his father are said to have been tense ever since he and his wife divorced last year. Both McCoys denied the rumor.

TUESDAY, JULY 18

Subject: greetings from the colonies
From: Mark
To: Patrick Stoughton

Hi Patrick,

The reality of how much my life has changed has finally hit home. It was easy to put it out of my mind while we were hiking around the Lake District, mainly because I was too busy trying not to lose sight of you in the fog. Now that I'm here with nothing more onerous to do than align my deck chair with the sun (sun: a bright star in the center of the solar system), I'm feeling a little stressed out. I guess it's not surprising given that I'm a single, unemployed 42 year-old man who has no idea what he's going to do with the rest of his life.

Mornings and nights are toughest. I wake up half expecting Keiko to come in with my morning cup of tea and then I realize that's never going to happen again. It's like being kicked in the gut. I strap on my armor and get on with my day and then when I go to bed it hits me all over again.

The scene here at Inglewood has been anything but restful. I was hoping that Catherine and Suzanne would have worked things out before I got here but it didn't turn out that way. My sister's got her knickers in an uproar, as you Brits would say. She can't put two sentences together without complaining about Suzanne. The way Catherine treats her is absolutely appalling, and although Suzanne must be seething, she refuses to rise to the bait. And that, of course, infuriates Catherine even more.

I enjoy a catfight as much as the next man but I'm doing my best to stay out of it. I don't doubt Suzanne is the rank opportunist Catherine claims she is - I told you about her adventure with one of my father's friends and now she's set her sights on a geek whose family owns half of Canada - but if that was the litmus test for social acceptance my sister would have to sever ties with just about everybody she knows.

The truth is Catherine has never forgiven Suzanne for 'stealing' Michael away from her, although she'll go to her grave denying that they were anything more than friends. I never knew exactly how Douglas felt about it. He had to know that he was Catherine's second choice, but their union was more of a merger than a marriage so perhaps it was never a question of having to swallow his pride. Then again, short of running away with the children, there's nothing he could have done to rile Catherine more than saddling her with Suzanne for the summer.

The way I see it, Suzanne couldn't have stolen Michael away if he wasn't ripe for the taking. No disrespect to my sister, but after lying beside that luscious body under a hot sun the past few days it's no mystery why Michael would have been attracted to her.

love to Deborah and the kids,

Mark

From: Patrick
To: Mark

Hi Marco,

Like the man said, nothing like a new bird to forget an old one … Ouch! Deborah's looking over my shoulder and the silly cow's just boxed my ears. She says I'm an insensitive lout, don't I know you're in mourning? As if that matters to wee willy.

Hi Mark. Deborah here. Don't pay any attention to Patrick. If he didn't have the sensitivity of a dimwitted gnat, he might be able to understand what you're going through.

P here: Begging the question of why my wife married such a lout instead of the chinless wonder she was going with when we met. A man so sensitive he cried when they went to see ET!

Deborah again. Blinded by pity as I am, I have obviously given Patrick too much credit. If he only *had* the sensitivity of a dimwitted gnat, he would have a better understanding of what you're going through. As to why I married him, I thought it would stop the whinging. I was wrong.

Subject: matchmaker, matchmaker
From: Maggie
To: Catherine

Hi Cat,

I had lunch today with Laura Robinson, and guess what? She has left her husband and is moving back here from Marin County with her eight year-old daughter. She's perfect for Mark - smart, sweet and as gorgeous as ever. What's more, the Thompson's have invited her to their cottage and she's going up to Lake Joe sometime next week. She was *very* interested to hear that Mark was there. I don't know if he'd remember her from the Lawn, she would have been a teenager when he went to Japan, but she certainly remembers him.

I'm not sure what happened with her husband, she didn't get into the details. I got the sense it was quite traumatic but the settlement she got must have helped ease the pain. Her ex sold his software company to Microsoft a few years ago. I don't know how many millions he got for it, but Laura must have ended up with a lot of them. I went through the listings with her and she wasn't interested in anything under three million.

I just want everybody to be happy.

Love,
Maggie,

Marjory Stern
Oak Tree Realty
Everything Maggie touches turns to SOLD!

From: Catherine
To: Maggie

Hi Mags,

Great news, and the timing couldn't be better. Mark's only been here a few days but everything I told him about Suzanne flew out of his head the moment he laid eyes on her. She's cast a spell on him using the same potion she used to bewitch Douglas: one part praise, one part deference, with a pinch of adoration and a generous dollop of cleavage. She's been careful to keep him at arm's length - she's not going to seduce him now, not while she's trying to reel in Gary - but as we both know, she's the kind of gal who doesn't go anywhere without a backup plan.

I saw Laura's sister Leslie a month ago at the club, and she didn't say a word about the divorce. And I thought my family was secretive! I only met Laura's husband once, at the wedding, but he struck me as the sleazy type. I'm sure she's well rid of him. I feel bad for her daughter, though. This kind of thing is always hardest on the children.

Let me know when Laura's coming up.

love,

Catherine

From: Suzanne
To: Lisa

Dear Lisa,

I am biding time at Inglewood until my prince returns. Gary's father is out of intensive care but he remains in hospital. His doctors suspect he has cancer but are awaiting test results before they can confirm the diagnosis. To think that Gary may soon be burdened with the responsibility that comes with owning a vast real estate empire elicited my most tender feelings, but when I expressed my condolences he cut me short, and told me that he will not pretend a grief he does not feel. He has not spoken much of their relationship but I gather that it has not been an easy one. As you know, his father is a religious man and Gary's failure to wholeheartedly embrace the faith has been a constant sore point with the old man.

Fortunately there is a new face at Inglewood to help me pass the time a very handsome new face. After fourteen years in Japan, Catherine's brother Mark has moved back to Canada. Life is so unfair. Not only did Mark get all the looks in the family, he also got all the wit and charm. Indeed, the contrast between him and his sister is so striking that DNA testing is called for.

He will be spending the rest of the summer with us, and I was pleased to see that he does not share his sister's antagonism towards me. I would not describe his attitude towards me as friendly - Catherine's hostility towards me is such that to do so would be tantamount to treason - but he has at least been civil and cordial, and I am confident that it will only be a matter of time until we become good friends. When a man in a Speedo and a woman in a bikini spend several hours a day in each other's company, it creates an informal environment that tends to break down any walls which may others may have put up.

That, of course, will anger Her Frumpiness, reason enough for me to do what I can to cultivate a friendship with Mark. Besides, as I have lost my enthusiasm for board games, I will need something to amuse me until Gary and I are reunited.

Love,

Suzanne

From: Lisa
To: Suzanne

I am pleased to hear that you are feeling more at home at Inglewood. But I feel compelled to remind you that walls have many functions. It is important to distinguish between a prison and a fort.

From: Suzanne
To: Lisa

Rest assured, my dear sister, that I am keenly aware of where my interests lie. I remain committed to Gary in body, heart and soul.

WEDNESDAY, JULY 19

Subject: bad news
From: Lisa
To: Suzanne

Dear Suzanne,

Eduardo has just given me the most terrible news. It appears
that your enemies are more hostile than you had imagined. You
may remember his short-lived crocodile farm from a few years
back, the one that ended in bankruptcy when one of the
creatures devoured a poodle owned by the wife of the Minister
of the Interior. Well, his former partner has just returned from
a visit to Toronto and told him he had heard a rumor that you
were having an affair in the months preceding Michael's death.

I strongly suggest that you consult with an attorney. This
vicious slander must not be allowed to spread unchecked. Do
you have any idea who might be responsible?

Your concerned sister,

Lisa

From: Suzanne
To: Lisa

Dear Lisa,

I was saddened to hear of the latest allegations about me. But not surprised. When this group smells blood, they go in for the kill.

I am grateful for your advice, and I would certainly consider legal action were the rumor not, unfortunately, well founded. By the time the affair - for want of a better word to describe a meaningless diversion with one of Michael's male nurses - began, my late husband lacked the energy to get out of bed, or do anything while he was in it, other than accept the advice of his cretinous broker. I was feeling, as you can imagine, lonely and neglected and very much in need of care. Who better to turn to than a member of a profession dedicated to caring for others?

I do not understand how word leaked out. I took exceptional care to be discreet, wanting, above all, to spare Michael the pain of being furious with me. Aside from the one time Victor and I met at a hotel - where we entered and left separately - we were never together outside of the house.

Although the rumor will undoubtedly reach Inglewood - gossip is the number one topic of conversation among Catherine and her friends excluding real estate, which is less a topic of conversation than a euphoria-inducing narcotic - I am confident it cannot be substantiated. Victor, the one person who could do so, was content with the generous gift I gave him when we parted company, and the possibility that he will be tracked down to his ancestral village in the Azores is too remote to concern myself with.

I hope you will not judge me harshly. Yours is the only opinion that matters to me.

Love,

Suzanne

From: Lisa
To: Suzanne

Dear Suzanne,

You don't have to defend yourself to me. We all have our own needs and we all do what we must in order to survive. I would never dream of judging you. If I had been forced to spend my childhood in the care of someone as dour and unloving as Tante Regina, my spirit would have been broken. That you were able to emerge with yours intact says volumes about your nature.

If anyone is to be judged harshly, it is I. I never told you this, but the university offered to defer my admission for a year after Mutti and Papi died so that we could all stay together. I turned it down because I couldn't bear the thought of staying in Tante Regina's house another minute. It was inexcusably selfish of me, and I have never forgiven myself. I will never forget the day I left, seeing you standing in the doorway as I got into the taxi, refusing to shed a tear even though your heart must have been breaking. You gave me a brave little smile, took your brother's hand, and then disappeared into that cold and inhospitable environment. You have never once reproached me for deserting you. For that I will always be your grateful and loyal sister.

Love,

Lisa

From: Suzanne
To: Lisa

There is nothing to reproach you for. Your love and support are the one constant in my life. The world can be an unforgiving place and I cannot tell you how comforting it is to know that there is one person who will always be on my side.

Subject: hello from Japan
From: Keiko Yamamoto
To: Mark

Dear Mark,

I hope you are well and enjoying life. Are you at Inglewood? I have very fond memories of the week we spent there so many years ago. It was so kind of your mother to leave the day we arrived so that we could have some time to ourselves.

I am sure you will remember Toru Hiroshami who owns the dry cleaning establishment around the corner from our apartment. He and I are seeing each other in a serious dating relationship. I tell you this because I do not want you to hear it from someone else.

Please give my most fond salutations to your mother and father, and to your sister and her husband.

I will always treasure the time we spent together.

With affection,

Keiko

From: Mark
To: Keiko

Dear Keiko,

I was delighted to get your email. I've been meaning to write you since our last telephone conversation. I was very sorry that it ended so badly and I want to apologize for accusing you of being dishonest with me. It's true, as you said, that you told me from the beginning that you were not interested in having children and I realize now that it had nothing to do with my not being Japanese.

I remember Toru well. I always admired how neatly he ironed my shirts. I am very happy for both of you. It is rare to find a Japanese man who does not want a family and you both must feel very lucky to have found each other.

I too will always treasure the time we spent together.

With affection,

Mark

THURSDAY, JULY 20

Subject: Laura R
From: Maggie
To: Catherine

Hi Cat,

I bumped into Leslie at Whole Foods and she told me that Laura is going up to the Thompson's on Saturday. She said the family is very relieved her marriage is over. They've been trying to get her to leave Todd for years. Turns out the prick had been cheating on her from day one, he kept promising he'd stop and she kept believing him. First great love and all that. She'd probably still be with him if she hadn't caught him in bed with her best friend! Doesn't that make you feel hopelessly provincial?

He promised it would be the last time, but this time she didn't fall for it. Leslie and her mother took turns babysitting her for a few months while they sorted through the legal stuff to make sure she didn't have a relapse. Todd went ballistic when she told him she was moving back here with their daughter. Leslie said he fought Laura for custody every step of the way, blew more than a million in legals even though his own lawyer told him he didn't have much of a chance. Apparently he's as good a dad as he is bad a husband, and the girl is crazy about him. Part of the reason why Laura put up with him for so long, I guess.

Leslie said that Laura's daughter was having trouble adjusting to the move. She misses her father and is angry at Laura for taking her away from him. It's been really hard on Laura but there's not much she can do except wait it out. She can't exactly tell an eight year-old that her beloved father is a first-class schmuck.

Leslie was thrilled to hear that Mark was at Inglewood. She asked for your number so don't be surprised if she gives you a call to strategize.

David and I are off to Knowlton today. Sans enfants! David's mother is taking care of them.

Love,

Maggie

Marjory Stern
Oak Tree Realty
Everything Maggie touches turns to SOLD!,

From: Catherine
To: Maggie

Hi Mags,

Just got off the phone with Leslie. If Mark and Laura are half as keen on the match as she and I are, it's a done deal. I called the

Thompsons and they're going to bring Laura and Cailin to lunch on Sunday.

I told Mark that Laura was coming up and he had absolutely no trouble remembering who she was. Funny how memory works, isn't it? He's probably forgotten people he met last week and yet he remembers a 5'10" blonde he hasn't seen in 15 years. Go figure.

Laura couldn't be coming at a better time. When I went down to the dock this afternoon I got the distinct impression that there was something going on between Mark and Suzanne. The two of them were ignoring each other in a decidedly unnatural manner and it made me very nervous.

You're leaving the kids with David's mother? Doesn't she have Alzheimers?

love,

Catherine

From: Maggie
To: Catherine

She does, but the doctors say it's not very advanced. And Zack has promised not to send her out for a walk like he did the last time she babysat.

Subject: getting any?
From: Patrick
To: Mark

Hi Marco,

Have you had your way with Suzanne? There is a significant wager at stake. If I'm right, Deborah has to dress up as a governess and give me the discipline a naughty schoolboy deserves. If I'm wrong, we get a new chesterfield.

P

From: Mark
To: Patrick

I'm afraid you'll have to put the cane back in the closet and pry your credit card from your wallet. I gave it the old college try, and got severely chastised by Suzanne for my troubles. Put an end to my fantasies, mundane as they may be by your perverted standards. She is determined to be true to her pygmy boyfriend.

I heard from Keiko. She's seeing a Japanese guy just like I predicted, although there's not much satisfaction in saying 'I told you so' to yourself.

Subject: virtue triumphs
From: Suzanne
To: Lisa

Dear Lisa,

My commitment to Gary has been tested and I am pleased to report that my virtue has emerged intact.

This morning, as Mark was putting sunscreen on my back, his strong capable hands strayed to areas not normally in need of protection from the sun's harmful rays. I discouraged the taking of such liberties, but not, admittedly, without a brief internal struggle. My physical needs have been sorely neglected ever since I put Victor on a plane to the Azores. My brief interlude with Henry is not worthy of mention; suffice to say that Viagra is not the miracle drug it is made out to be. And, as you know, my relations with Gary have yielded only an anticipatory pleasure.

Nonetheless I told Mark to cease and desist, reminding him that I was already spoken for. My appeal to his better nature was met with the glib reply that this could be "our little secret, the dwarf never has to know." I suppressed a chuckle lest he think I was amused by his insulting gibe, and not by his laughable ignorance. With limbs that are in perfect proportion to his body, any educated person would know that Gary is a midget not a dwarf.

I was deeply offended that Mark believed me capable of such casual deceit, and told him so. He then had the effrontery to question the depth of my feelings for Gary, describing him, redundantly, as a "little gnome" whom I could not possibly be in love with. I allowed my gaze to travel the length of his lithe 6'2" frame before staring directly into the aquamarine eyes that soften his ruggedly attractive features and, summoning up all the haughtiness I could muster, told him that, as he clearly had no idea of the qualities that attract a woman to a man, it was no surprise that he was unattached.

I later wondered how one would precisely define a gnome, and laid a silent wager with myself that Gary would be able to satisfy my curiosity, if nothing else.

The results of the latest tests have confirmed that Gary's father has pancreatic cancer. They are doing more tests to determine if it has spread, but the doctors have told Gary to prepare for the worst. Gary has decided to stay by his father's side. It is a wise decision. With everything he has at stake it would be foolish to give the old man reason to question his devotion.

Suzanne

From: Suzanne
To: Mark

Dear Mark,

I hope you have no hard feelings about today. I know how difficult it is to be all alone but don't lose hope. With seven billion people in the world, there surely must be one for you.

Have you considered joining Facebook? I am sure it would not be long before you found many new friends.

Best,

Suzanne

From: Mark
To: Suzanne

Dear Suzanne,

thanks for the kind words. makes me quite ashamed for thinking you didn't care.

best

mark

MONDAY, JULY 24

Subject: we're back
From: Maggie
To: Catherine

Hi Cat,

We're back from Knowlton. We had a fabulous time. It's the first holiday we've had on our own since Emma was born. We missed the kids like crazy, of course - until we were about an hour outside of the city and realized how blissfully quiet it was in the car. Now I understand why boarding schools are so popular.

The kids had a fantastic time with their grandmother. They amused themselves by seeing how many times they could get her to give them dessert until she caught on.

How did it go with Mark and Laura?

Love,

Maggie

Marjory Stern
Oak Tree Realty
Everything Maggie touches turns to SOLD!

From: Catherine
To: Maggie

Hi Mags,

Laura and Cailin came over yesterday and you're right, she's
absolutely perfect for Mark. I took to her immediately. We got
along so well that I was even able to forgive her for being so
young and beautiful. She absolutely charmed Douglas as well. A
few questions about that damned composting toilet of his, and
she had him eating out of her hand.

Things between her and Mark were a little tense at first because
of Cailin. Leslie wasn't kidding about the girl having trouble
adjusting to the divorce! Whenever Laura and Mark started
talking, she would interrupt and demand her mother pay
attention to her. It was very awkward for Laura but she was
extraordinarily patient and understanding. My mother would
have been horrified - in her books there is no crime greater than
indulging a child, especially if it's a girl - but I thought it was
very wise. If the child needs reassurance, then for God's sake
reassure her.

Fortunately Cailin spent most of the day in the water with Cleo
and Tony - they could tell the girl was upset and went out of
their way to be nice to her, I was so proud of them - which gave
Mark and Laura a chance to talk. It was a little embarrassing at
first, everyone knew that the purpose of the lunch was to
introduce them, but once they relaxed they got along fine.

Today they're taking Cailin to the fair in Port Carling. Laura's
very nervous about it, but Mark's so good with kids - Tony and

Cleo simply adore him - that I'm sure she'll be eating out of his hands by the time they get back.

Suzanne didn't have the decency to absent herself despite knowing that James Thompson is one of Henry's best friends. She hung around the entire time like a barnacle, although few barnacles would be brazen enough to prance around in the flimsy piece of material she laughably calls a bikini. Everybody, including Mark I was delighted to see, ignored her.

I'm not sure what's going on with her and Gary. He no longer calls every day, and when he does, their conversations are short and not so sweet. Makes me wonder if the blush is off the romance. Perhaps now that he's sampled the goods, he's decided not to buy. She's being very brave about it but I can tell she's upset. I've tried to show her how concerned I am by periodically asking if she has heard from Gary but it's clear the gesture isn't appreciated. I'm beginning to doubt that we will ever be friends.

Love,

Catherine

From: Maggie
To: Catherine

Glad to hear Mark and Laura got off to a good start despite Cailin's antics. It's absolutely wonderful how sensitive Tony and Cleo were to her. It's a credit to the way you and Douglas have brought them up. My brats think only of themselves. It's bad enough that I have to drive Zach to an arena in Mississauga every weekday for practice, I have to go there Saturday and Sunday as well because he's been invited to an all-star camp run by one of the Maple Leafs. If you think it's occurred to the little ingrate to say thank you, think again.

Interesting about Gary and Suzanne. David told me he heard that McCoy senior is so infuriated by Gary's divorce that he's considering giving his shares in the company to his church. Maybe junior has finally realized that a dalliance with Suzanne is not the best way to reassure the old man that he's on the road to redemption.

A pity things don't seem to be working out for our old friend. Her house has been on the market for six months now and she hasn't received a single offer. With Gary out of the picture, she must be desperate to sell. Hmm.

Talk soon,

Maggie

Marjory Stern
Oak Tree Realty
Everything Maggie touches turns to SOLD!

From: Catherine
To: Maggie

Hi Mags,

Whatever possessed Gary to think that consorting with Suzanne was a good idea in the first place? That's baffled me from day one.

Poor you having to wait around a draughty hockey rink all summer. It's a shame that kids are forced to specialize at such a young age these days, and have to give up the rest of their childhood, especially when only a handful end up making a career of it. We're so lucky not to have that problem. Tony has so many interests and I think he would be miserable if he had to give any of them up.

Love,

Catherine

TUESDAY, JULY 25

From: Suzanne
To: Lisa

Dear Lisa,

I have had only the most cursory communication with Gary in the last week. I am trying not to read too much into it - he has much on his mind - but I fear that the time and energy I have invested in this little man have been for naught. I can't stop myself from wondering if word of my indiscretion with Victor has reached his father's ears. If that's the case, my fate is sealed.

The waning of his ardor has not escaped Catherine's notice. Regular as Tante Regina's cuckoo clock, she pops up to ask if I have heard from him, with a sympathetic look on her face so transparently false that it can have no purpose other than to convey her satisfaction at the way events are unfolding.

At the same time as my own romance is stumbling, another has begun to bloom here at Inglewood - between Mark and a young divorcee named Laura Robinson who is visiting at a neighboring cottage. She is admittedly attractive, slim and blonde, but there is a certain laziness to her features that does not bode well for the future. Although Mark seems eager to pursue the relationship, I predict his interest will soon fade. Laura is blessed with a very sweet disposition, but her failure to reveal a personality beyond an insipid pleasantness leads me to believe she does not have one. As Tante Regina used to say when someone was described as 'nice': "What does that mean? That she doesn't spit in her tea?" Mark is a man with appetites, and they will not be satisfied by a woman who has none of her own.

If Mark has found favor in Laura's eyes, he has not been as well received by her five-year old daughter Cailin whose opinion may prove to hold more sway than her own. Cailin harbors hopes her parents will reconcile and sees Mark as an impediment to that dream, and my early observation is that her mother is disinclined to go against her daughter's will.

Today she and Mark took the girl to a magic show in a nearby town. The magician needed an adult volunteer for one of his tricks and brought Mark onto the stage. Cailin started yelling at the magician to "make him disappear, make him disappear," and when the magician failed to comply, she had a temper tantrum on the spot.

Love,

Suzanne

From: Jean
To: Catherine

Darling,

Laura should never have let Cailin get away with her outburst at the magic show. As soon as the girl realizes that she has no choice in the matter, she'll accept Mark and move on. I do hope she isn't one of those modern mothers who cater to their child's every whim out of some misapprehension that to do otherwise would scar them forever. Parents who have an inflated view of their influence on their children are not doing them a favor. As your pediatrician told me when you were a toddler, "children thrive in spite of their parents."

Daddy was delighted to hear about Mark and Laura. He and her father were in the same year at UCC and he says Gordon is the salt of the earth, which coming from him is high praise indeed.

I have just heard some very interesting news about Suzanne. Norman Kennedy told daddy that the little tart was having an affair while Michael was on his deathbed. Norman heard about it from his brother who said his daughter-in-law got it from a friend. Nobody knows the identity of her partner-in-crime, but the two of them were caught in flagrante delicto in a washroom at the Royal York. I'm generally leery of rumors, but in my opinion this one passes the sniff test.

Mummy

From: Catherine
To: Maggie

Hi Mags,

I know how much you detest gossip, but I simply must pass this little tidbit along. I just got an email from my mother who heard that Suzanne was amusing herself with a lover while Michael was dying. The two of them were caught doing it in the washroom at the Royal York. Totally outrageous, even for a woman who is constitutionally incapable of keeping her legs together, but it has the indisputable ring of truth.

Love,

Catherine

From: Maggie
To: Catherine

Fascinating news about our old friend. Far be it from me to add fuel to the fire, so if you don't want to know who she was shtupping, best to stop reading now.

Still there? It was a male nurse who was taking care of Michael. Her real estate agent told me a few months ago, just before Michael died. I didn't pay much attention at the time - he's not the most reliable source and even for Suzanne it seemed beyond the pale. Guess I gave her too much credit.

Marjory Stern
Oak Tree Realty
Everything Maggie touches turns to SOLD!

From: Catherine
To: Maggie

Let's not lose sight of the fact that these are unproven allegations that have the potential to ruin the little that is left of Suzanne's reputation so please keep this to yourself, and a couple of hundred of your closest friends.

SATURDAY, JULY 29

From: Suzanne
To: Lisa

Dear Lisa,

Just when I feared that all was lost, Gary called this morning with a most unexpected message: his father wants to meet me. I must confess the prospect makes me nervous. As much as I abhor the exaggerated emotions of melodrama, I am convinced that my future hangs in the balance. Gary scarcely takes a breath without his father's say so, and if I do not receive his blessing I will surely be shown to the door.

Time is weighing heavily on the old man and his insistence on meeting me tonight left Gary and I time only to review the basic principles of Christian dogma. He was surprised I was so well versed, as was I. The lessons I thought long forgotten came flowing back, as did the memory of those endless hours spent at the kitchen table under Tante Regina's vigilant gaze.

Gary has asked me to wear "something conservative" for the meeting and gently suggested my wardrobe was not up to the task. I asked him to be more precise, but the only guidance he offered was to say that if the outfit would find favor with the Pope, it would likely not offend his father.

Yea, though I walk through the valley of the shadow of death, best not to do so in high heels and a plunging neckline.

Love,

Suzanne

From: Lisa
To: Suzanne

The image of you in a nun's habit has brightened a dismal day.

I am sure your meeting with Gary's father will go well. I know that if you turn your mind to it, you can make a favorable impression on any man. Eduardo echoes my sentiments. He has spoken to his mother about your situation and she has assured him that your dreams will be fulfilled.

Love,

Lisa

From: Catherine
To: Maggie

Hi Mags,

It's only been a week but Laura and I had a heart-to-heart last night, and I am very optimistic that things are going to work out between her and Mark. They are certainly on the same page when it comes to raising family. Laura feels it's crucial that Cailin have a sibling, and the sooner the better. She's very encouraged by the way the girl has warmed up to Mark in the last couple of days - no more temper tantrums and she has even let him take her out in the canoe a few times. And although she didn't say so, I think she hopes that moving ahead quickly with Mark will make it easier for her to forget about Todd. She doesn't like to talk about it, but it's obvious the bastard broke her heart.

None of this is for public consumption. Laura said Mark would be very upset if he knew she'd talked to me. She said he resents the fact that we never accepted Keiko and that he would be put off if we are too enthusiastic about her. It was very perceptive of her and made me even more convinced that she and Mark are a good match.

I'm glad to see him being so practical for once in his life. I hate to sound like my mother, but relationships that are founded on common interests and mutual respect are the ones that tend to last. No matter how passionate two people are when they first meet, that kind of passion only lasts in the movies. Not that the physical side isn't important, Douglas and I still do it once a month, regular as clockwork. When he turns off the tv before the news comes on and tells me to come to bed, I know it's time to close my eyes and think of George Clooney

Love,

Catherine

PS. Judging by Suzanne's demeanor when she returned this afternoon from her meeting with Gary's father, things did not go well. She was so discouraged that she walked by the hallway mirror without stopping to look at herself, and has yet to emerge from her room. My guess is that the old man gave Gary an ultimatum: show her to the door or forget about becoming a real estate mogul.

From: Maggie
To: Catherine

David's a twice-a-month man - according to the Talmud it's supposed to be once a week but he's only half-Jewish. My cue is when he gargles with mouthwash before he comes to bed. Time to close *my* eyes and think of cheesecake. I used to keep them open but all I could think about was that the ceiling needed repainting.

Great news about Mark and Laura. I'll keep my fingers crossed.

Maggie

PS. Head's up. If you hear a piercing shriek from Suzanne tomorrow morning, don't worry. It just means that her agent will have passed on the ridiculously lowball offer I will be instructing my client to make.

Marjory Stern
Oak Tree Realty
Everything Maggie touches turns to SOLD!

From: Suzanne
To: Lisa

Dear Lisa,

I have just returned to Inglewood after meeting Gary's father, and I fear I did not find favor in the old man's eyes.

I met Gary in the lobby of the hospital, attired in a shapeless dress no Amish woman would be ashamed to wear. We rode the elevator up to his father's room in silence - that Gary did not recount the circumstances surrounding its invention was an indication that he was as nervous as I.

Cautioning me to speak only when spoken to, Gary opened the door to his father's room. I knew the cancer was far advanced, but I was not prepared for the ghostly figure that greeted me: his eyes - two burning coals above a long white beard - the only sign of life. Gary suggested we put our hands together and pray, but the old man ordered him to leave the room.

He motioned me to his side. "You spent the night at my son's cottage," he intoned, and looked at me as if I were the whore of Babylon. The accusation took me by surprise, and I reacted without thought. The arrogance of this old man, to think he had the right to judge me. I stared into his fierce eyes and declared that I had nothing but contempt for his old world morality, and for the men who preached it. "If God indeed exists," I said - my lack of faith received a fiery look – "*her* desires" - I was rewarded with another spark of rage – "are beyond the understanding of mortal men. The dictates of my conscience and not your righteous moral code, will guide my actions."

He did not respond to my diatribe - by the time I finished speaking, he had drifted off - but it surely did not please him. He looked so peaceful lying there. I could not help but think that there could be no better time for God to have mercy on his soul. And in so doing take mercy on my own.

When I returned to Inglewood I went down to the dock where I chanced upon a scene that did nothing to improve my mood. Mark was regaling Laura with a stroke-by-stroke account of his latest round of golf, while Cailin sat complacently on his lap, giggling in foolish delight every time he interrupted his narrative to pluck a coin from behind her ear.

This tableau of false domestic bliss drove me to my room where a letter from Jennifer awaited. It was our first communication in the three weeks she has been at camp and, I was not entirely surprised to learn, camp has not been to her liking. In defiance of the laws of probability, her two hundred fellow campers are, to a girl, "retarded losers" whose idea of a good time is to march through the forest singing camp songs for hours on end, led by a cadre of fascist lesbian counselors. This, of course, is all my fault, and the only way I can make it up to her is to send her to school in Lausanne next year with her friend Zoe.

Although I bear no ill will toward the Swiss, nothing would give me more pleasure than to accommodate her request. But that, barring divine intervention, sadly appears to beyond my reach.

Love,

Suzanne

SUNDAY, JULY 30

From: Suzanne
To: Lisa

Dear Lisa,

I just received a depressing call from my real estate agent informing me that we had received an offer for the house at $100,000 under the list price. It's outrageously low but after last night's fiasco with Gary's father, I am out of options. With no income coming in, I can no longer afford to make the mortgage payments. I told the agent I wanted to think about it, but there is really nothing to think about.

They say that it is in adversity that we reveal ourselves. I am about to find out who I am.

Love,

Suzanne

From: Lisa
To: Suzanne

Dear Suzanne,

Eduardo and I want you to know that you and Jennifer are
always welcome here at Casa Blanca. Eduardo has spoken to his
mother and she says you are welcome to stay in the casita. It is
very private and has a lovely view of the ocean. Your dollars
will go much further here than in Toronto, and there is an
excellent and inexpensive private school nearby where Jennifer
can complete her high school education.

Love,

Lisa

Subject: divine intervention
From: Suzanne
To: Lisa

Dear Lisa,

Thank you for the kind invitation. Please tell Eduardo, and his
mother, how much I appreciate their offer. However, I have
just received a phone call from Gary that gives me reason to
believe my hopes are still alive.

I have done Gary's father a grievous wrong. In rebuking him for
judging me, I have committed the very transgression I had

accused him of. When the old man awoke today, he summoned Gary to his side and informed him that although I know not how to curb my tongue nor contain my ire - heinous faults in a woman - God has put me on this earth for a reason and it is not his place to question his maker's will.

Gary would not tell me what God has in store for me. He is coming to Inglewood this afternoon so that we can discuss it face to face. But I cannot resist the urge to speculate, and thus far have been unable to imagine a scenario other than the one that has been in my mind since the happy day we met.

In a bid to distract myself until he arrives, I spent some time perusing the "Inglewood Almanac," a set of embossed leather journals written by Grandpa Jack that date back to 1927. Although they did not provide me with anecdotes of the early days of cottage life with which I could regale my prince, I found in them the origins of Catherine's sparkling wit. July 2: *Rained some in the morning. Cleared up in the afternoon.* July 3: *Rained all day.* July 4: *Hot and sunny. 94 degrees at 6:30 pm.*

My curiosity thus satisfied, I went down to the dock where Mark had just emerged from his daily swim across the lake. "An hour and 25 minutes there and back," he said, looking at his watch and pointing to the distant shore. "Not bad, if I say so myself." "Wow," I gushed, and asked if he had walked or swum. He chuckled and then began doing pushups, positioning himself in front of me lest I miss the show. Up and down he went, how many times I do not know or care, I lost count at 47, and all the while I was laughing to myself. Did he really think I would be impressed by such a puerile act? The blood that surged into those bulging muscles had clearly been diverted from his brain.

He had barely finished his exertions when Gary called to confirm the time of his arrival. My joy did not escape Mark's notice, and he inquired about the status of my "merger with the troll." I allowed that it was progressing more quickly than anticipated. He offered me his most sincere best wishes. Like Mutt and Jeff, he said, Gary and I are a perfect match. No more than he and Laura, I replied, if one believes that Ken belongs with Barbie.

Love,

Suzanne

From: Jean
To: Mark

Dear Mark,

Daddy and I were very pleased to hear from Catherine that you are seeing Laura Robinson. I don't mean to criticize but I do wish you would tell us these things yourself. We had dinner last night in Monte Carlo with the Ryans. They are friendly with the Robinsons and had heard about you and Laura, and it would have been very embarrassing if we had not known about it.

Love,

Mummy

From: Mark
To: Jean

I wouldn't make too much out of this. Laura's a lovely woman but we've been seeing each other for less than a week so it's a little early to start printing up the wedding invitations.

Subject: Mrs. Gary McCoy
From: Suzanne
To: Lisa

Dear Lisa,

My premonition was correct. Gary asked me to marry him and I have accepted, though ours will be a marriage in name only.

My single-minded pursuit of financial security has blinded me to what, in retrospect, ought to have been glaringly obvious. My dear fiancé is gay. Our marriage is a subterfuge to reassure his father that he is a righteous man, and thus a worthy successor to his fortune. In that latter desire, at least, we are as one.

Gary has known he was gay since the age of four when he became intoxicated by the sights and smells in the locker room at the YMCA. He knew his father would not accept this was God's will. Leviticus 18:22: "Thou shall not lie with a male as with a woman; it is an abomination," was one of the old man's favorite passages, and one his son was obliged to learn by heart.

His secret came to light when he was in high school. He and his drama teacher were apprehended in a storage room enacting the title roles in an avant-garde production of Romeo and Juliet that culminated, not with that frustrating double suicide, but with the happy ending that all lovers seek. The older man was deemed the villain of the piece, and duly sacrificed, but Gary's father knew his son was no unwilling dupe. The years of counseling which followed were deemed a success when Gary married Sonia and sired their two boys. But their divorce has awakened his father's dormant fears.

Hence my summons to the old man's bedside. I misinterpreted his motives in asking about my sleepover at Gary's cottage. He was not accusing me of wanton behavior, he wished to confirm that I had slept with his son. My impassioned outburst laid to rest his suspicions that Gary had returned to his deviant ways.

The old man does not have long to live, and he wants to see us married before he dies. It did not take Gary and I long to come to an arrangement. There was some give and take - he gave, I took - but in the end we both agreed that a ten million dollar lump sum payment and five million dollars a year was fair value for my services.

We are driving to Toronto tomorrow to meet our lawyers, and if all goes according to plan, my future will be secured before the day is done. My sole concern is the health of Gary's sainted father. I pray the Lord keep him by our side - at least until we have signed the prenuptial agreement.

Love,

Suzanne

MONDAY, JULY 31

Subject: man proposes, God disposes
From: Suzanne
To: Lisa

Dear Lisa,

We like to think we are masters of our fate but we have no more control over our destiny than a puppet dancing on a string.

Gary was in a buoyant mood on the drive to Toronto this morning. He held no rancor at being bested in our negotiations and even graciously suggested how I might best structure my windfall to minimize my income tax obligations.

When we arrived at my lawyer's office, he confirmed that the documents were in order. I signed two copies of the agreement and as I slid them along the table to Gary, his cell phone rang. If only the call had come a minute later …

I was privy only to Gary's side of the conversation, but from the look of fright etched on his face and his constant repetition of the phrase "yes father," I was not entirely taken by surprise when he hung up and told me he was reneging on our deal.

It took some time, between his sniveling bouts of self-pity and the vitriol he directed at his ex-wife, for the explanation to emerge: Sonia had just left the hospital after presenting his father with indisputable proof that Gary had not abandoned his deviant ways. The proof was in the form of a burly construction worker who moonlights as a gentleman's companion and was able to identify Gary as one of his regular clients.

Sonia advised the old man that if Gary did not give her sole custody of their sons, she would make his sexual proclivities public by means that included a letter to the members of his church. A single sentence was all it took for him to convince Gary to accede to Sonia's demands: "I will not entrust my fortune to a soldier in Satan's army."

Gary then announced that he had to leave for the airport to catch a flight to Chicago, whence he will fly to Wichita, Kansas where his father has enrolled him in a workshop entitled "Don't be gay, choose the other way." We had only a few moments to say our final goodbyes. He told me how sorry he was that things worked out the way they did, and I told him how sorry I was that he was such a pathetic excuse for a human being.

I walked out of my lawyer's office full of self-pity, but it was not long before I felt myself free of the heaviness that has enveloped me these past few weeks. My mind has embraced what my heart has known for some time, that my pursuit of a man for whom I feel such indifference was poisoning my soul. I am well rid of this tedious and irksome bore.

Love,

Suzanne

From: Lisa
To: Suzanne

When one door closes, another opens. Perhaps at Inglewood?

From: Suzanne
To: Lisa

You have given voice to my unspoken thought.

TUESDAY, AUGUST 1

From: Suzanne
To: Lisa

Dear Lisa,

I drove to Inglewood today, intent on telling Mark that I had ended my relationship with Gary, and hopeful that he would not be indifferent to the news. Catherine was in the kitchen, rooting through the freezer, when I arrived. As she liberated a vat of ice cream from its frozen lair, I told her that Gary and I had parted ways. A look of satisfaction crossed her face, whether at my information or her find I cannot say, and spoon in hand she then conveyed the news that tore my world asunder. Mark and Laura are engaged.

I mulled this over at some length while Catherine polished off her sugary treat - if only her announcement had been as easy to digest - but I could not avoid the dismal truth. Wherever my future might lie, it will not be found here. I told Catherine that I would take my leave tomorrow. Even if she were a prisoner on death row, and I the governor granting a reprieve, I do not think I could have given her more joyful news.

Love,

Suzanne

From: Catherine
To: Maggie

Hi Maggie,

Suzanne returned to Inglewood today, alone. Gary has finally come to his senses and given the poor dear her walking papers. She's being very plucky about it, even tried to convince me that it was her decision.

You should have seen the look on her face when I told her that Mark and Laura were engaged. She was absolutely crushed. I actually felt a twinge in my heart, for a moment I thought it was sympathy but then I realized it was the chili I had for lunch.

She's leaving tomorrow. Call me. It's no fun gloating by myself.

Catherine

From: Maggie
To: Catherine

I have just advised my clients to renew their offer - at $200,000 under list. Very fair, I think, given current market conditions.

Marjory Stern
Oak Tree Realty
Everything Maggie touches turns to SOLD!

From: Mark
To: Patrick

Hi Patrick,

Major developments at Inglewood. Laura and I are engaged - sort of.

She's as eager to have a child as I am - she doesn't want Cailin to be an only child - and we both agree there's no point in waiting. We won't actually get married unless she gets pregnant, but since the parental units wouldn't be thrilled with that arrangement, we decided we to tell everyone we are engaged.

I know this is all happening ridiculously quickly but I don't see that as a problem. Neither of us has unrealistic expectations about the relationship. We've both gone down the falling in love route and it hasn't worked out for either of us. It's a fantasy anyway, how can you love someone you don't know? I believe true love is something that develops over time, it takes patience and understanding and good will, and there's no reason why Laura and I can't have that.

I'm ready for your scathing British wit, so fire away.

Mark

From: Patrick
To: Mark

Not my place to judge, but I do have two words of advice.
Pre Nup.

Subject: Greetings from Canada
From: Mark
To: Keiko

Dear Keiko:

I am writing to tell you that I am engaged to be married. I am
telling you because I didn't want you to find out from anybody
else. My fiancée's name is Laura Robinson. She is divorced and
has a lovely eight-year old daughter. She is a wonderful mother,
and is eager to have more children. Like most women, she says
motherhood has been the most rewarding and meaningful
experience of her life.

I hope you and Toru are well, and that his dry cleaning business
is doing well.

With affection,

Mark

From: Keiko
To: Mark

Dear Mark:

I was very happy to get your letter and to see that you have found someone as perfect as Laura. You know I want you to be happy, but your news made me happy as well because it makes it easier for me to tell you my news.

Toru and I are going to have a baby. I don't know how this happened - you know what I mean - but now that it has I am very happy. Even though my baby is still in my stomach, I know that what Laura says about being a mother must be right. Last week I felt it move inside me for the first time. Toru cried with joy when he felt the baby kick. It kicks so hard I am certain it is going to be a boy.

With affection,

Keiko

From: Suzanne
To: Lisa

Dear Lisa,

The situation is bleak and I have but one arrow left in my quiver.

Mark returned this evening and after congratulating him on his impending nuptials, I told him that I had terminated my relationship with Gary. He said he was surprised, he had no idea that McCoy Development was on the verge of bankruptcy. When I pressed him to explain this puzzling comment, he said he could think of no other reason why I would set Gary free. I disregarded the insulting implication, and explained that although Gary was a kind and decent man, relations between us lacked the ardor I could not - would not - live without. It was not my place, I said, to judge those who choose to marry, not for love, but to satisfy a pitiful desire to give meaning to their empty lives by perpetuating their feeble genes, but I for one, would rather live out the rest of my days alone than endure a dull and passionless marriage.

He seemed to take my words to heart, and as we sat there, he waiting for Laura and Cailin to arrive, and I pondering my uncertain future, I could not help but wonder what course our lives would take were a ten-ton logging truck and Laura's Mercedes to suddenly occupy the same position on the space-time continuum.

Laura and Cailin arrived in the midst of this idle speculation. Cailin demanded Mark take her out in the canoe, which gave Laura and I a chance to talk. I commented on the remarkable reversal in her daughter's attitude towards Mark. Laura took full blame for her daughter's earlier intransigence. She said she had been ambivalent about the termination of her marriage, and had sent mixed signals to the girl. She went on to say that she has now accepted that Todd - her ex - didn't love her, and the insight has allowed her to move on. Last night she told him that she and Mark were engaged - it would be an understatement to say he did not give his blessing to the match - and with that announcement has put the past behind her.

I sensed in her both yearning and regret. In her mind her marriage may be over, but I do not think her heart has followed suit. Indeed, from the bitter way in which she talked about her ex, I am convinced that she is still in love with him.

I feel it is my duty to give that love a chance to bloom.

Love,

Suzanne

Subject: Cailin
To: Todd Sullivan
From: Suzanne

Dear Todd:

I am Catherine Roger's sister-in-law, and a guest at Inglewood where I have met Laura and Cailin. I am writing because I am concerned about the welfare of your daughter.

I don't know if you are aware of how traumatized she has been by her separation from you. I know it would break your heart, as it did mine, to hear the plaintive tones in which Cailin bemoans your absence. Can a child utter four words sadder than "I miss my daddy?" And now, of course, with Laura's engagement to Mark, the situation will only worsen and I fear she will not emerge unscarred.

I know you want your daughter by your side so that you can provide her with the paternal love every girl so desperately needs. Despite the fact that Laura is now engaged, the relationship you yearn for is not beyond your reach. You have perhaps, amid the acrimony of the recent past, lost sight of the power you have to touch your ex-wife's heart. Laura is still in love with you, and although that love lies dormant, if she believed you loved her too, I am convinced that it would be awoken.

If that is of any interest to you, please allow me to be so bold as to propose a course of action. I suggest you begin by calling Laura and apologizing for the way you reacted when she told you of her engagement. Tell her that you wish her well, and that you want to see her one more time to say goodbye.

Do not plead your case until you meet, and when you do, begin by telling her that the responsibility for the failure of your marriage is yours, and yours alone. Allow her to recite the wrongs she feels you have done her. I can assure you that she will not pass up the chance to do so. Do not defend yourself, even if the charges are unjust. Wait until she has exhausted all her grievances, and then, and only then, tell her that you love her still. She is your sun, the center of your universe. That is the theme to be elaborated upon. There is no need to strive for originality of expression. The tritest phrase, uttered with the proper feeling, will come across as fresh.

You must next convince her of your willingness to change. I know that issues of fidelity have arisen in the past. This is no concern of mine, it is not my place to judge you, but as a woman I can tell you that a promise to reform will not suffice. Tell Laura that you are prepared to go into counseling.

Finally, do not, under any circumstances, refer to your wish to be reunited with your daughter. This will not reassure Laura that she is your reason for living.

Yours sincerely,

Suzanne Braun

From: Todd
To: Suzanne

Hi Suzanne,

Thanks for putting me in the loop. I knew Cailin was having a rough time but I didn't know it was this rough. I can't bear the thought that my little girl is suffering. She is the best thing that ever happened in my life and I have been miserable without her. Since she was born, I spent as much time with Cailin than Laura did, maybe more, and if the legal system wasn't so tilted against men, she would never have been allowed to take her to Canada in the first place.

I spoke to Laura and she has agreed to meet me for lunch tomorrow. I'll take your advice on how to deal with her but winning her over is going to be a tall order. There's a lot of water under that bridge. I won't say I was the perfect husband but she has never acknowledged that it takes two to tango, she's always blamed me for everything that went wrong in our marriage, she never once wondered why I felt the need to look elsewhere.

Todd

From: Suzanne
To: Todd

This isn't going to work if you don't take complete responsibility for the breakdown of the marriage. One excuse and you'll be lunching by yourself.

From: Todd
To: Suzanne

Not to worry. Just venting. I'll make sure to order the humble pie.

WEDNESDAY, AUGUST 2

From: Maggie
To: Catherine

Elisa told me she saw Laura and Todd having lunch at the Courtyard. What gives?

Marjory Stern
Oak Tree Realty
Everything Maggie touches turns to SOLD!

From: Catherine
To: Maggie

This is the first I've heard of it. I called Leslie but she didn't know anything about it either. She's in a total state of panic, and she put me in one too. She's positive Todd is going to persuade Laura to give him another chance. She said she'll call as soon as she finds out what's happening. I'll keep you posted.

From: Suzanne
To: Lisa

Dear Lisa,

It appears my arrow missed its mark and I will be leaving
Inglewood tomorrow. Thank you for your generous offer to
join you and Eduardo at Casa Blanca. The prospect of a fresh
start is appealing, and if it were up to me alone, I would be on
the next plane to Argentina. But I fear Jennifer will not be of
like mind, and if she were forced to come against her wishes,
you and Eduardo would soon regret the invitation.

Love,

Suzanne

From: Catherine
To: Jean

Dear Mummy,

I just heard from Leslie and all is well. Laura told her that Todd
did try to convince her they should get back together. He
pulled out all the stops - said she was the center of his universe,
that life wasn't worth living without her, the snake even offered
to go into counseling. Laura didn't fall for it. She told him that
she and Mark were engaged and the sooner he got used to the
idea, the better. He's flying back to California tonight. Laura's
dropping him off at the airport on her way up here.

Suzanne was in the room when I got off the phone with Leslie and as it would have been rude of me not to share the reason for my joy, I did. I suppose it was silly of me to think that she would be interested. After all what is Mark to her? Absolutely nothing - now that Todd's gambit has failed. Her reaction confirmed my suspicions. She went straight up to her room where, unless my ears are playing tricks on me, dresser drawers are being emptied. I think I'll go up and offer to help her pack. It would be rude of me not to.

Love,

Catherine

From: Jean
To: Catherine

Darling,

Wonderful news. I have to admit that Daddy and I were quite worried. Can you imagine how embarrassing it would have been for us if Laura had gone back to Todd?

I spoke to Adele yesterday. She and Gordon are over the moon about Mark and Laura. Don't breathe a word of this to Mark. God forbid he should know he is making us happy.

Love,

Mummy

THURSDAY, AUGUST 3

From: Catherine
To: Maggie

Hi Mags,

Leslie told me she passed on the awful news. This has turned into a trainwreck. It took Mark exactly one nanosecond to make a beeline for Suzanne. When I woke up in the middle of the night to go to the bathroom, I heard the two of them going at it. They disappeared after breakfast and haven't surfaced since.

He can't be serious about her, can he?

Catherine

From: Maggie
To: Catherine

Hi Cat,

Whoa! You're getting way ahead of yourself. Let's examine the facts. What have we got here? An eligible bachelor desperately looking for a wife and an amoral siren in search of a meal ticket.

Just kidding! You've got nothing to worry about. That tired old damsel in distress routine may have worked with an old man like Henry, but Mark will see through it in a minute. I'm sure he's just having fun.

If things do get out of hand, try putting ricin in her coffee. Tasteless, odorless, and fatal. But you didn't hear it from me.

Marjory Stern
Oak Tree Realty
Everything Maggie touches turns to SOLD!

From: Laura Robinson
To: Mark

Dear Mark,

Thank you for being so understanding. You have every right to be furious with me but, like you said, we're both better off this way. We've known from the start that we weren't right for each other and it would have been a big mistake to carry on.

I have no idea if I'm doing the right thing, Todd has broken my heart more times than I can count, but I know if I don't give us one more chance I'll regret it for the rest of my life. I'm still not sure how it happened. He was very nice all day, none of the anger I was so used to seeing - he even said he'd go into counseling, which he had absolutely refused to do in the past -

but I never considered changing my mind, not even as I was driving him to the airport. When I dropped him off he gave me this sad little look, said he would always love me, that all he wanted was for me to be happy, and that if it couldn't be with him then he hoped it would be with you.

Then I realized he hadn't said a word about Cailin the entire day. I guess that's what did it. I had been so positive that was his motive. I told him to get back in the car. I must be out of my mind.

By the way, I always appreciated how you pretended you weren't interested in Suzanne whenever we were all together. Didn't fool me for a minute but it was very sweet. I'm not sure she deserves you but that's not for me to say. I didn't deserve you either.

You're a good man.

best,

Laura

From: Suzanne
To: Lisa

Dear Lisa,

Good news for those who treasure family values. Laura and Todd have taken the first steps towards the reconciliation that will ease their daughter's troubled soul. Mark conveyed the happy news to me last night. He candidly admitted that he was much relieved that his relationship with Laura had come to an end, and confided that it had never sat well with him. Referring to my reasons for ending things with Gary, he acknowledged that his longing for a passionate relationship was as deep-seated as my own, and as we then discovered, no less urgent.

Although we decided to wait some time before publicly revealing the new nature of our friendship, from the disgusted look on Catherine's face when we joined her at breakfast this morning it was clear that we had given the game away. She was so discouraged that she left her stack of pancakes untouched. I sensed she was struggling to come to terms with this new development and in order to give her time alone to deal with it, I asked Mark if he would like to see the etchings in my room. He knows full well that there is no artwork there, other than the photograph of Grandpa Jack standing beside his newly finished outhouse, but he bounded from the table without a word. Our communication is that finely tuned!

Denial, anger, bargaining, depression and then, if all goes well, acceptance. These are the stages of the grieving process. As I followed Mark upstairs, the sound of china shattering on the kitchen floor satisfied me that Catherine had reached the second phase of her journey where, I suspect, she may yet linger for a while.

Love,

Suzanne

From: Lisa
To: Suzanne

I am pleased that you are once again so full of life. I hope that this will prove to be more than a summertime adventure.

From: Suzanne
To: Lisa

Your hope is mine.

Subject: Laura and I
From: Mark
To: Jean

Dear Mother,

I wanted you to hear this from me first. Laura and I have ended our engagement. She's back with her ex-husband, or at least she's going to see if she can work it out and frankly she has my blessing. We don't love each other and it would have been a big mistake to go through with the marriage.

Mark

From: Jean
To: Mark

Dear Mark,

Thank you for telling us about you and Laura. Dad and I are disappointed things didn't work out but the last thing we want is to see you in an unhappy marriage. If sometimes we seem a little overbearing, it's only because we want the best for you.

Love,

Mummy

From: Jean
To: Catherine

Darling,

Call Jake Onrot and ask him for the name of the best private detective in Toronto. We need to find the male nurse Suzanne was consorting with while Michael was dying.

I will not have that woman as my daughter-in-law.

Mummy

FRIDAY, AUGUST 4

Subject: Suzanne Braun
From: Ambler Detective Agency
To: Jean Rogers, Catherine Rogers

1. I spoke to Mr. Norman Kennedy, the initial source of the claim you have hired me to investigate. He put me in touch with his brother's daughter-in-law, Ruth Jensen.

2. Ms. Jensen reported that she received the information about Ms. Braun's affair from Cheryl Hutt, whose company, Urban Delights, catered a party at Ms. Jensen's house at which Ms. Braun was a guest. The party was held on February 16 of this year, two days prior to the death of Ms. Braun's husband.

2. Ms. Hutt told me that one of her waiters, Carlos Alvarez, was the source of her information. Ms. Hutt said that Mr. Alvarez, who also works as a room service waiter at the Royal York Hotel, recognized Ms. Braun at the party and told her that: "I saw that broad at the hotel yesterday doing some dude in the washroom."

3. This morning I spoke to Mr. Carlos Alvarez who provided the following information:
- He works part-time as a room service waiter at the Fairmont Royal York Hotel.

- At Ms. Jensen's party he recognized Ms. Braun as a hotel guest to whom he had delivered a bottle of champagne the previous afternoon.
- When he entered the hotel room Ms. Braun was lying in bed wearing a negligee.
- The door to the washroom was ajar and he observed an unknown male, wearing only a towel, shaving.
- Mr. Alvarez identified a photo of Ms. Braun as the woman he saw in the hotel room.
- He described her male companion as good-looking, dark-haired and of medium height and build.
- After Ms. Braun signed for the champagne, Mr. Alvarez left the room and had no further contact with Ms. Braun or her companion.

4. The Nightingale Nursing Centre provided nursing care for Ms. Braun's husband. I should have a list of the nurses who took care of him in a day or two. I will keep you posted.

Eric Ambler
President
Ambler Detective Agency

Subject: got your message
From: Patrick
To: Mark

Hi Marco,

Deborah told me you called. Glad to hear you and Laura called it off. Life's too short to spend it with someone you don't love. Suzanne sounds more your type.

Deborah said she got the impression that Suzanne wasn't someone you would take seriously, that you were only interested in having some fun. "You say that as if it's a bad thing," I made the mistake of commenting. Oh well, I sleep better on the couch.

We're off to Ibiza tomorrow - if we're still talking. I'll be in touch when we get back. I, for one, hope you're having fun.

P

From: Mark
To: Patrick

hey,

I'm having a great time with Suzanne. After so many years with Keiko, I'd forgotten that a woman could be this lusty. She's got a great sense of humor, too. At breakfast today I said I was so hungry I could eat a horse. She whinnied. Lady Catherine was not amused. If her lips were any more puckered, you'd have to wrap a pair of panties around them.

Tell Deborah that I'm siding with you on this one. I'm not ready to jump into anything right now, and although Suzanne hasn't shown any interest in my portfolio - yet - knowing her history I suspect it's just a matter of time, I can't say I care.

Like the song says, 'Boys Just Wanna Have Fun.'

Have a great time in Ibiza.

Mark

Subject: Paul
From: Lisa
To: Suzanne

Dear Suzanne:

I just got a call from Paul. He was worried because he hadn't heard from you in a while. He didn't know you were going away for the summer, email service in Darfur being about as reliable as you'd expect. I gave him your new cell phone number. He said he had to go to a meeting but would call you in an hour or so.

I don't know how he does it, dealing with that misery day after day. You would think that he would be burnt out after all these years, but he was as laid back as ever. And yes, he's still single. Plus ça change.

Love,

Lisa

From: Suzanne
To: Lisa

Dear Lisa,

I just got off the phone with Paul. I can't tell you how wonderful it was to hear his voice again. Nobody makes me laugh like he does. The IRC has been in touch with him - again - about the job in New York but he turned it down - again. It took all my self-restraint not to scream at him to take it, but he's so damn stubborn that I knew that would only make him dig his heels in.

There is an outside chance we might get to see each other this summer. There's a conference on the refugee situation in Toronto in August and Paul's executive director thinks she'll be too busy to go which means Paul will take her place. He says he should know in a day or two. Keep your fingers crossed.

Love,

Suzanne

MONDAY, AUGUST 7

Subject: Suzanne Braun
From: Ambler Detective Agency
To: Jean Rogers, Catherine Rogers

Further to my report dated August 4:

1. There were two male nurses on the team that cared for Ms. Braun's husband: Victor da Silva and Stefan Gorchov.

2. This morning I interviewed Mr. Gorchov. He is openly homosexual and I have eliminated him as a possibility. He told me that Mr. da Silva no longer works for the agency, and has returned to his home in the Azores. As he and Mr. da Silva worked different shifts, he had no information regarding his relationship with Ms. Braun.

3. Mr. Gorchov described Mr. da Silva as "a real hunk, a Mediterranean Brad Pitt." He said he was in his early 30's, lean and muscular, with black curly hair. This description is consistent with that given by Mr. Alvarez of the man he saw in Ms. Braun's hotel room.

4. I have contacted my subagent in Lisbon who has advised that da Silva is the Portuguese equivalent of Smith. He says it will be extremely difficult to find him and has asked for authorization

to put more men on the job. Before I can proceed further, I will need direction from you regarding the financial limits to be placed on the investigation.

Eric Ambler
President
Ambler Detective Agency

From: Jean Rogers
To: Ambler Detective Agency, Catherine Rogers

Spare no expense.

From: Paul Brown
To: Suzanne

Hi Suze,

Looks like I won't be coming to Toronto after all. The ED's decided to go to the conference. I'm really disappointed.

Love,

Paul

From: Suzanne
To: Paul

Are we never going to see each other?

From: Paul
To: Suzanne

My offer stands. You and Jennifer can always come live with me.

From: Suzanne
To: Paul

My answer stands too. Move the refugee camp to the Riviera and I'm in.

FRIDAY, AUGUST 11

From: Patrick
To: Mark

Hi Marco,

Deborah and I just got back from Ibiza. We stayed at the same hotel where we honeymooned and, if I say so myself, we did ourselves proud. We're both completely knackered and in desperate need of a holiday.

Hi Mark. Deborah here. I don't know if it was the sun or the Rioja, but Patrick was a beast. Not that I'm complaining. I had a smile on my face the entire time: the comedy channel ran Fawlty Towers nonstop. Thank God for cable tv.

P: Pay no attention to her, I never do. How are things going with Suzanne?

From: Mark
To: Patrick

Things are going great with Suzanne. better than great. The truth is I fell for her the moment I saw her and the more I see of her, the more I like what I see.

I suppose I was gun shy about getting seriously involved because of her escapade with Henry, but I should have known there are two sides to every story.

Suzanne didn't want to talk about it, getting the details out of her was like pulling teeth but when they emerged it became clear that he is an extraordinarily venal and despicable old man who took advantage of a widow's grief, and then, when his perverted will was thwarted, dragged her name through the mud. My interpretation, not hers. She insisted that she was the one to blame when she was guilty of nothing more than telling the truth. Nearly broke my heart to see her beat herself up like that.

I've never felt like this about anybody. Mock me if you wish. I can take it.

Mark

From: Patrick
To: Mark

Sounds like the real deal, but my advice is the same.
Pre Nup.

Subject: Mark
From: Suzanne
To: Lisa

Dear Lisa,

The past week has flown by. Mark and I have spent virtually every minute in each other's company, and I cannot remember when I was last so content.

We are well matched in every way, and I have good reason to believe that his attitude regarding the future is already beginning to shift. Tonight the dear boy told me he loved me, a declaration uttered, not impetuously in the heat of passion, but considered, in its wake.

I credit this welcome development to a recent conversation about my unfortunate experience with Henry. From certain remarks Mark let fall, it was clear that his opinion of me had been infected by the slanderous accusations that have been bandied about by all and sundry. I could not let this go unchallenged. Unless he believed my feelings for him were unsullied by financial considerations, I knew we would be destined to share only the fleeting pleasures of the flesh and the union of our two bodies would not be coupled with the fusion of our souls.

I resolved to make no attempt to justify my actions. I had erred in accepting Henry's advances and I would not hesitate to admit it. Nor would I make an appeal for Mark's sympathy. I would merely present the facts and let him come to his own conclusions.

And so I recounted how, after nursing my beloved husband of eighteen years through a long and debilitating illness, I was left lonely and bereft. And how, while in this fragile state, I had met Henry, who seemed a kind and gentle man, and in the depths of my despair agreed to marry him. I related how, when I regained my emotional equilibrium and realized that I had mistaken gratitude for love, I told Henry that I could not marry him. I recalled his fury when I returned his engagement ring.

It was at this point in my narrative that the painful emotions triggered by these recollections broke down my determination to remain dispassionate. Holding back my tears as best I could, I told Mark how Henry had sworn to destroy my name and my reputation. By now I could not stop the tears from flowing, and in between my sobs I explained how he had distorted the nature of our normal prenuptial negotiations to his advantage, portraying me, a naïve woman unschooled in the ways of the world, as an unscrupulous opportunist, and he, the seasoned businessman with a lifetime of experience to rely on, my hapless victim.

That was the plain unvarnished truth. Either Mark would accept the version given by an angry and vindictive old man whose pride had been wounded, or he would believe a woman who had lost everything but her integrity by following her heart.

The tears that welled in his eyes told me all I had to know.

Love,

Suzanne

Subject: our contract
From: Mark
To: Jeffrey Goldberg

Hi Jeff,

My accountant told me July's payment hasn't been paid, and that you aren't returning his calls. I don't want to believe you're screwing me over, but what else can I think?

Mark

From: Catherine
To: Jean

Dear Mummy,

Things have gotten worse since we spoke. Mark is definitely in love with the little vixen. He went to town this afternoon to meet with his lawyer about his deal with Jeff, and from the way he and Suzanne said goodbye to each other, you'd have thought he was going off to war.

Love,

Catherine

From: Jean
To: Catherine

We can't pin our hopes on Ambler. It's been nearly a week and he still hasn't found da Silva. We've got to do something now or it will too late.

Call me!

SATURDAY, AUGUST 12

From: Suzanne
To: Lisa

Dear Lisa,

I have just received some devastating information. Mark has been betrayed by his former business partner, and is on the verge of bankruptcy.

This morning he went to town to meet his lawyer to discuss the deal but as he did not appear to be seriously vexed, I assumed that it was of no great import. But I have just overheard a phone call between Catherine and her mother that casts the matter in a different light. Mark's former partner has cheated him out of his share of their business, and his only recourse entails a lengthy and uncertain journey through the Japanese legal system. Furthermore, his father, whose hostility towards me has sharpened since he learned that Mark and I were keeping company, has threatened to disinherit him unless he severs our connection, and that, as Catherine regretfully advised her mother, her brother will not do.

Mark's refusal to bow to his father's dictates does him credit, but the fact remains that he is not the man I thought him to be. Although it does not do me proud to admit it, I cannot say this has not influenced my feelings towards him. I have feelings for him I have had for no other man, but no love can be said to be true until it has been tested by adversity, and I will not pretend that mine could pass that test.

Suzanne.

Subject: Victory is ours!
From: Catherine
To: Jean

Dear Mummy,

It worked like a charm. We both deserve to win an Oscar. I had barely hung up when Suzanne rushed past me and ran upstairs. I heard her on the phone making a reservation at the Sheraton. Mark's due back for dinner but my guess is she'll be long gone by then

Catherine

From: Lisa
To: Suzanne

Dearest Lisa,

I hope you are sitting down as what I am about to tell you will come as quite a shock. My bags were packed and I was ready to return to Toronto when tears, unbidden, began streaming down my face. There was nothing I could do to stop the flow. I could deny my heart no longer, I am in love with Mark, and beside that truth his reduced circumstances matter not.

I feel a sense of wellbeing in his company, and a delight when I am in his arms that I have felt with no other man. It feels strange to say I love him, but I do. It will feel stranger still to tell him so.

Love,

Suzanne

From: Lisa
To: Suzanne

Dearest Suzanne,

I cannot tell you how pleased I was to hear you express your love for Mark, and how long I have hoped that this day would come. You closed your heart to the world when Mutti and Papa were taken away and I did not know if the day would come when you would open it again.

People speak too easily of transformation, they bandy the term about as if all that is required is a change of diet. But it takes courage and self-awareness to truly transform oneself, to reverse a lifetime of conditioning. I am so very proud of you.

I believe this article I found on the Internet will add to your happiness. It will also serve as a reminder not to let down your guard against your enemies.

Love,

Lisa

News of The Day

TOKYO. July 2. Mark Rogers, President and co-founder of Global Funds (Japan) Inc., a boutique investment firm specializing in business services acquisitions, has sold his share in the company and resigned from the company's board of directors. Rogers and co-founder Jeffrey H. Goldberg launched the firm 13 years ago. Its holdings have grown by an impressive 20% annually and are now estimated at $985,000,000.

Rogers is leaving Japan to return to his native Canada to pursue other opportunities. "It's been a great run," Mr. Rogers said, "and I'm very proud of what Jeff and I have accomplished. It really came down to whether I was wanted to relocate permanently to Japan and when push to came to shove, I just wasn't prepared to make that decision."

Rogers sold his shares back to the company for a reported $43,000,000. To allay investors concerned about the effect of the sale on the company's cash flow, only one-third of the purchase price was paid on closing, with the balance to be paid over the next 5 years. "Mark was the driving force behind the company and he'll be sorely missed," said Goldberg. "But our association is by no means over. We've got a joint venture in the works with a French partner and having Mark located in North America will be a big plus."

From: Suzanne
To: Lisa

Thank you for the article. I printed out a copy so that I could refer to it at will, but I seem to have misplaced it. It's possible I left it on the vanity in Catherine's bedroom.

Subject: Re: Our contract
From: Jeff Goldberg
To: Mark

Hi Mark,

Good to talk to you yesterday. Again, my apologies for not getting back to you sooner. My accountant said he wired the funds to your bank this afternoon. Let me know if they didn't arrive.

Marilyn couldn't believe it when I told her that Keiko was pregnant. After all she put you through! She figures that's why Keiko never visited her in the hospital, she was too ashamed Jean-Phillippe is delighted you are interested in moving ahead. The IP issues are very complicated so we'll need to bring the lawyers in on this. He suggests a conference call tomorrow at 3 pm your time. Let me know if that works for you and Ivan.

Jeff

From: Mark
To: Jeff

I'm the one who should apologize. I should have spoken to you before jumping to conclusions. I'm just glad that Marilyn got a clean bill of health. It must have been a terrible month for you and the kids.

Tomorrow at 3 is fine. Talk to you then.

Subject: Suzanne Braun
From: Ambler Detective Agency
To: Jean Rogers, Catherine Rogers

Further to my report of August 5: My agent in Lisbon has located Victor da Silva in the town of Povoação. He is on his way there now and will meet with him tomorrow morning.

Eric Ambler
President
Ambler Detective Agency

SUNDAY, AUGUST 13

Subject: Suzanne Braun
From: Ambler Detective Agency
To: Jean Rogers, Catherine Rogers

Re Suzanne Braun

1. My subagent met with Victor da Silva and his attorney, Mr. Elpidio Leite, this morning in the town of Povoação.

2. Mr. da Silva confirmed that he had an affair with Ms. Braun. He said it began approximately three months before Ms. Braun's husband passed away and ended a month of so afterwards, when Ms. Braun terminated the relationship.

3. Mr. da Silva has no letters, photographs or any other documentation that can independently confirm what he told me. However, he did provide very specific details of the affair that could only be known to someone who was intimate with Ms. Braun.

4. He is willing to provide an affidavit with those specifics in exchange for the sum of US$ 50,000, which is to be wired to his lawyer's account.

If you would like to proceed, please let me know and I will send you the banking information.

Eric Ambler
President
Ambler Detective Agency

From: Jean Rogers
To: Ambler Detective Agency, Catherine Rogers

Good work. I will have my banker contact you first thing tomorrow (Monday) morning to make the arrangements.

From: Ambler Detective Agency
To: Jean Rogers, Catherine Rogers

I have informed Mr. Da Silva's attorney that we are prepared to meet his terms and my agent has arranged to meet him and his client tomorrow to sign the affidavit.

Yours truly,

Eric Ambler
President
Ambler Detective Agency

Subject: disaster
From: Suzanne
To: Lisa

Dear Lisa,

Disaster has struck again and this time there will be no escape.

This afternoon, as Mark was about to leave to Toronto for another meeting with his lawyer, Catherine joined us, and flush with pretended consternation, related that she had "something terrible" to tell us. A "vicious rumor" that I had an affair with one of Michael's nurses had reached her ears.

I dismissed it with a scornful laugh intended to suggest that I would not dignify this farfetched tale with a denial. Mark took the news less calmly. He insisted that Catherine attempt to locate the source of this ugly slander. For his part, he would discuss the matter with his lawyer to determine how best to proceed.

I thanked him for his concern but requested he refrain, suggesting that we ought not to wallow in the mire with petty minds capable of such wicked invention. He begged to disagree. If this vile lie were allowed to spread unchecked, he said, it would reflect badly on my reputation and he insisted that I permit him to protect it.

After Mark left, Catherine informed me that a detective hired by her family had located Victor at his home in the Azores, that he had been very forthcoming, and that his affidavit setting out the details of our 'sordid affair' would soon arrive.

Tears welled up in my eyes and I did not have the strength to stop them. I threw my dignity aside and begged Catherine to show compassion, if not to me, then to her brother whose love for me she surely could not deny. It was a waste of breath. There was no spark of humanity in those beady eyes, just the brutal indifference a lion shows its prey. "I'll say goodbye to the children for you," she said, and waddled out of sight.

Suzanne

From: Lisa
To: Suzanne

If Mark truly loves you, he will forgive you for your indiscretion.

From: Suzanne
To: Lisa

Indiscretion is perhaps not quite the right word to describe what occurred between Victor and me. I have spared you the details but his affidavit most assuredly will not. Suffice to say that when all is revealed, Mark's love for me, as strong as it may be, will surely wither. He is a proud man and will not humiliate himself by allying himself with a woman who so outrageously cuckolded her dying husband.

From: Catherine
To: Jean

Dear Mummy,

I broke the news to Suzanne. She begged me not to tell Mark. The short version is that I said no. The long version involves much weeping and gnashing of teeth but I can't possibly do it justice until we speak in person.

She is - finally - leaving Inglewood tomorrow.

love,

Catherine

MONDAY, AUGUST 14

Subject: Suzanne Braun
From: Ambler Detective Agency
To: Jean Rogers, Catherine Rogers

<u>Re Suzanne Braun</u>

1. My agent met with Mr. da Silva's attorney, Elpidio Leite, this morning. He was informed that Mr. da Silva refuses to talk about his relationship with Suzanne Braun and does not wish to be contacted about the matter.

2. Mr. Leite made it clear this isn't a tactic to extract more money. He said that his client called him this morning to say he'd changed his mind. He apologized for initially accepting the offer, and explained that he had not thought things through. He is engaged to the mayor's daughter and if word of the affair got out, not only would the marriage fall through, he would be publicly disgraced and forced to leave his hometown where his family has lived for generations.

3. My agent naturally promised that the information would be held in the strictest of confidence but as Mr. Leite pointed out, there is no way to guarantee this.

4. Mr. Leite has instructed his bank to return the payment to the sender bank.

Eric Ambler
President
Ambler Detective Agency

From: Jean
To: Catherine

Darling,

This is the worst possible news. Daddy is positively livid. He vows he will disown Mark if that woman is still there when we arrive at Inglewood. I told him that will only serve to push Mark away but he is as inflexible as a rock. Nothing I can say will change his mind. I am distraught beyond words. I have waited all these years for my baby to return home, and now I am going to lose him again.

Mummy

From: Catherine
To: Jean

Dear Mummy,

You don't have to worry about losing your baby. Nobody has to know about Mr. da Silva's change of heart. Suzanne came to me this morning and asked me to let her be the one to tell Mark about the affair. It was so very noble of her that I couldn't refuse provided, of course, that she agree not to tell Mark that we had hired Ambler. You and I know that we had his best interests in mind but I doubt he would agree.

I am going to celebrate with a bottle of Dom Perignon. You and daddy can put the $50,000 you just saved into the kids' education fund.

Love,

Catherine

TUESDAY, AUGUST 15

From: Suzanne
To: Lisa

Dear Lisa,

I could not get to sleep last night. I tossed and turned, unable to free my mind from the painful knowledge that I had come so close to realizing my dream, only to have it torn from my grasp. I was consumed by anger - not at Catherine and her mother who have never wavered in their desire to be rid of me - but at Victor's treachery, and in the early morning hours I called to tell him so.

He was unrepentant. He explained that Catherine's family had offered him to pay him for his cooperation and that, although he had no wish to harm me, he was about to be married. He hoped I understood that he had to put his family first. I told him that I understood only that I had treated him with generosity, and that he had repaid me with betrayal. I was expounding on this theme with some degree of passion, when Victor interrupted and said there was a way to make things right. I agreed - a public recantation followed by self-immolation would do the trick. Victor chuckled, and then presented an alternative solution. He had not yet signed the affidavit, nor would he do so, provided I could match the $100,000 that had been promised him.

I readily assented, and with our business now concluded, I congratulated him on his upcoming marriage. Fortune has smiled on my dear Victor since we parted. He is engaged to the mayor's daughter, and his future father-in-law has made him inspector of tourist facilities, a well-paid sinecure that in a town that attracts few tourists will require little of him.

I told him I was happy to hear of his good luck and, referring to my fond memories of our time together, jokingly suggested that I would be happy to provide him with a written reference to assure the mayor that his daughter's physical needs would be well taken care of. He laughed, if somewhat nervously. Unable to resist the urge to tease him further, I told him that for an appropriate fee - $100,000 was the amount that came to mind - I would refrain from corresponding with His Honor. A few moments of silence passed before he muttered his assent, and then our telephone connection was terminated.

I returned to my bed and fell into a deep and restful sleep. I awoke refreshed, and went to tell my host that I would be staying on at Inglewood. I found her on the veranda, a flute of champagne in hand. I have rarely seen her so animated and so joyous: eyes sparkling, brow unlined, a playful smile on her lips. She poured a glass for me, and offered up a toast in honor of my departure.

I then relayed the gist of my conversation with Victor. The light in her eyes went out, the furrows in her forehead re-appeared, the corners of her lips once more drooped downwards. At that very moment, Mark arrived and, taking note of the champagne, inquired as to the cause of the celebration. I explained that

Catherine had traced the origin of the accusations against me and discovered that it was all due to a misunderstanding so trivial as to not bear repeating.

Love,

Suzanne

FRIDAY, AUGUST 18

Subject: Suzanne
From: Mark
To: Jean

Dear Mother,

I'm sure that by now Catherine has told you about me and Suzanne. It doesn't take a psychic to guess what she has been saying about her. I hope you recognize it as the ranting of a deranged lunatic. If you want me to cite chapter and verse, here's a prime example. The other day she claimed someone told her that Suzanne was having an affair while Michael was on his deathbed. I called her on it and of course it turned out to be nothing more than a figment of her malicious imagination.

I hope father won't let his friendship with Henry color his view of Suzanne. Henry has many good qualities but a lack of vanity is not one of them. His pride was hurt when she dumped him, and he lashed out at her. Did that wrinkled old prune really think a beautiful young woman could fall in love with him?

When you meet Suzanne you will see that she's a remarkable woman and I expect her to be treated with respect.

Mark

From: Jean
To: Mark

Dear Mark,

Please don't think that we have prejudged Suzanne. I'm aware that your sister has personal reasons to dislike her and Daddy has made a point of asking me to tell you that he never believed Henry's situation with Suzanne was as clear cut as he presented it. If he hasn't indicated this before, it was only because of the loyalty he feels for a man he has known for nearly half a century.

So please don't worry, darling. We will treat Suzanne with the same hospitality we accord to every guest at Inglewood. We just want you to be happy.

Love,

Mummy

From: Jean
To: Catherine

Darling,

I have been wracking my brain to find a solution to our troubles. Without success. The sad truth is that I don't know how to get rid of her. What I *do* know is that if we openly express our disapproval of Suzanne, it will only push your brother deeper into her clutches. He has always favored forbidden fruit.

I'm still kicking myself for the way I treated Keiko when he brought her over to meet us. I don't know what possessed me to give her a book on The Rape of Nanking or to thank her for the 'house coat' when she gave me that exquisite silk kimono. I don't think Mark has ever forgiven me.

There's no use crying over spilt milk, but the least I can do is learn from my mistakes. I don't know how much of Suzanne's appeal can be explained by the pleasure Mark gets in pushing my buttons, but the only way to find out is to remove that factor from the equation and hope that without that distraction he will see her for the shallow and vain opportunist that she is.

I have assured Mark that Daddy and I will accept Suzanne - Daddy hasn't changed his mind but has agreed to cooperate for the time being - and you will have to do the same. I hate to ask you to do this - I know it's horribly unfair - but you have to apologize to Suzanne for the way you have treated her. Try to remember that the apology isn't for her, it's for Mark. I know it's asking a lot of you but unless you come up with a magic potion that can make that woman disappear, we really don't have a choice.

Love,

Mummy

From: Catherine
To: Jean

I will never apologize to that woman. I can't believe you and Daddy even asked.

From: Jean
To: Catherine

Darling,

Daddy and I can certainly understand how you feel. You have every moral right to refuse.

Before you decide how to handle the situation, we think you should know that under the terms of our wills, you and your brother will each have the right to force Inglewood to be sold. It would be a shame if, after close to a century, Inglewood were to no longer belong to the family, but you should do what you think best.

Love,

Mummy

Subject: Jean-Philippe
From: Jeff
To: Mark

Hi Mark,

I told Jean-Philippe we could meet this month, forgetting that it's illegal for a Frenchman to work in August. He suggests meeting in Paris on September 18. Does that work for you? We would need the proposal by the end of the month. That would give us plenty of time to make whatever changes are needed.

How are things going with Suzanne?

Jeff

From: Mark
To: Jeff

Hi Jeff,

The 18th is fine for the meeting and the end of the month is fine for the proposal.

Suzanne is coming to Paris with me, which I guess answers the question of how things are going with us. I can't wait for you to meet her. She is an amazing woman and I feel very lucky to have her.

My parents are coming around. I wouldn't say they're ecstatic about it, but they can see the writing on the wall and have decided to make the best of things. I don't know how, but they've managed to persuade Catherine to go along. After dinner tonight she apologized to Suzanne for the way she has treated her. It was a halfhearted apology but I could see that Suzanne was willing to accept it for the sake of preserving the peace. I wasn't about to allow that to happen so I stepped in and made sure that my sister sufficiently humbled herself to make up for the abysmal way she has acted. It turned out to be a very enjoyable evening.

Love to Marilyn and the kids,

Mark

From: Suzanne
To: Lisa

Dear Lisa,

It has been the most wonderful day.

After the children went to bed, Catherine announced that she had something she wanted to say to me. "I'm very sorry for the way I've treated you," she said, in a tone of voice that utterly belied her words. I waited for her to continue. Instead she reached for the bottle of wine that is never far from her side and topped up her glass, her mission apparently accomplished.

I could feel my anger rising up. Did she actually expect me to accept this insincere confession? Before I could say a word, Mark asked her what, exactly, she was apologizing for. "You know," she said, fluttering a chubby hand in the air by way of explanation. "I don't," he said in a steely voice that was music to my ears.

He led her through her transgressions one by one: the petty envy that led her to oppose my marriage to Michael; the childish grudge that drove a wedge between him and Douglas; the malice that led her to spread the slanderous accusations about my relationship with Henry - and then a pill she found most difficult to swallow - the spite that prompted her to accuse me of betraying my late husband without a shred of proof.

"We need never speak of this again," I said, when she was finally purged of all her sins. I held my hands out to Catherine. She stood and grasped my hands in hers. Her manner was both warm and reserved - 'we can be friends,' it seemed to say, 'though it may take some time to put the past behind us.' Then she clasped me to her doughy chest, and fiercely whispered in my ear "let's have no illusions, there can be no peace between us while I am still alive." "You have given me something to look forward to," I murmured in response. We straightened up, and with the ground rules thus established, smiled sweetly at each other. Mark beamed with joy. The malice in the air flew below his crude masculine radar.

Love,

Suzanne

SUNDAY, AUGUST 20

Subject: Jennifer
From: Suzanne
To: Lisa

Dear Lisa,

Will my troubles never end? As soon as one crisis is averted, another rears its ugly head.

I have just received a phone call from Jennifer's camp director. It appears that my darling daughter has not adapted well to camp life. She has shown no interest in canoeing, sailing, swimming, horseback riding, theatre, arts and crafts and the numerous other activities that have happily occupied generations of campers. Instead, she has chosen to amuse herself by seducing the head of maintenance, and for her troubles has been expelled from camp.

I will have to bring her to Inglewood, a prospect that fills me with dread. Mark has somehow - perhaps from comments I may inadvertently have made - formed the impression that Jennifer and I have a loving mother-daughter relationship. I have done nothing to disabuse him of this notion but it will not take Jennifer long to rectify this oversight. Indeed, once she discerns my intentions towards Mark, she is certain to devote herself to frustrating them.

I cannot say that she will not succeed. Mark is eager to experience the joys of parenthood and I have given him no reason to think I am not willing, or able, to make the journey with him. But a day or two with Jennifer will surely give him cause to wonder if I am fit to be the mother of his child. He and I have much in common, but when it comes to the debate of nature versus nurture, we stand in different camps. I have known, since I first sensed her foreign presence in my womb, that she is the spawn of Satan. I fear that Mark, although he may not say so, will blame me for the devil's work.

Love,

Suzanne

From: Catherine
To: Maggie

Hi Mags,

There is a glimmer of hope on the horizon.

I just got a call from Joanne. She told me that Jennifer has been kicked out of camp for having sex with the entire maintenance staff. Suzanne's on her way to pick her up right now. She told Mark that Jennifer was homesick and that after all that the poor girl's been through, she couldn't stand the idea of her suffering a moment longer. He bought it, of course. As far as he's concerned, every word Saint Suzanne says comes straight from God. Even her you-know-what smells like roses.

She's managed to convince him that her life won't be complete until she has once again experienced the joys of motherhood. The other day the Black's came by with their four month-old granddaughter. Suzanne asked if she could hold her and then made googly eyes at her for an hour or so until Mark left to go for his swim. The moment he was out of sight she handed the girl back as if she had the plague.

Unless he's completely brain dead which, sad to say, is a distinct possibility, the charade will come to an end once he gets a look at Jennifer in action. I wouldn't be surprised if the little vixen tries to seduce him just to see the expression on her mother's face. My guess is that after two days, three max, he'll realize that he'd be better off with a crack addict as the mother of his child.

Should be fun watching Suzanne try to tap dance around this.

Catherine

Subject: Back at Inglewood
From: Suzanne
To: Lisa

Dear Lisa,

It has been quite a day.

On the way to Jennifer's camp, I rehearsed the arguments I intended to use to convince the director to reconsider her decision. Jennifer was with her in the office when I arrived, and with the first words that tumbled out of her mouth, I knew I would not get a chance to plead my case. "Tell the stupid dyke to give me back my property," she demanded.

The charge of theft must be, it seemed to me, a blatant lie. I could not imagine how Jennifer's possessions could be of interest to this rugged woman. There was, I wagered, no thong under those knee-high bermuda shorts, nor a lace bra underneath that plaid shirt. Her crew cut would have no need for Jennifer's white truffle luxury conditioner. Yet the camp director did not deny the accusation.

The mystery was soon explained. The purloined item of which my daughter spoke was a videotape of the exploits which led to her expulsion from camp.

There being no reason to delay our departure any longer, we set out for Inglewood. As curious as I was to learn more of Jennifer's recent experiences at camp, I focused my attention on the more pressing task at hand - persuading her not to lay waste to my relationship with Mark. It is her nature to want to make me miserable, and as I did not expect her to renounce it, I decided to appeal to her self-interest.

I presented her with the two choices that she now faced, and asked her to select the one she thought would serve her best. Under what I termed the "peace treaty" scenario, she could improve her mind by studying at school in Lausanne where she would be reunited with her best friend Zoe, fortify her body with ski vacations in the Alps, and prepare for the responsibilities of adulthood by managing a $2,500 monthly allowance. I had only just begun to describe the "declaration of war" scenario when Jennifer confided that it has been her lifelong ambition to learn how to speak Swiss.

What happened next persuaded me that I have had more influence on my daughter's character than I had thought. Jennifer announced that although she agreed, in principle, to my proposal, there were some details that required further negotiation. She would need her own apartment, as the tumult of residence would make it impossible to concentrate on her studies. A car would therefore be necessary so that she would not be late for class. With groceries to pay for, the proposed allowance was hopelessly inadequate, and would have to be doubled. There were a number of other demands that I cannot remember at the moment, but as she insisted on reducing our agreement to writing, it will be an easy matter to refresh my memory.

Love,

Suzanne

SUNDAY, AUGUST 27

From: Suzanne
To: Lisa

Dear Lisa,

Jennifer has been here for a week and my fear that my precious daughter would not uphold her end of our bargain has proven to be unfounded. That is not to say that we have not had the occasional dispute about its terms. For example, she contends her obligation to refer to me as "mommy" is a public one, and that in private she can fall back on historical endearments such as "idiot" and "moron." Similarly, when the two of us are alone, she feels no need to employ all five fingers when she waves in greeting; she is content to brandish a single, upraised digit. But these are minor quibbles on my part, and as they have not altered Mark's favorable opinion of my parenting skills, I have not made an issue of them.

My relationship with Mark has benefited from the peaceful interlude, and I am increasingly at ease with the depth of my feelings towards him. He left today for a camping trip with friends and although I have not yet found the courage to tell him that I love him, I intend to do so when he returns.

I am going to Toronto tomorrow to see my doctor. I've been

nauseous the past few days and have some pain in my stomach. At first I thought it was caused by the unending stream of grilled cheese sandwiches, hotdogs and hamburgers which Catherine insists on serving up. Apparently congealed grease evokes nostalgic memories of the carefree days of yesteryear she is always droning on about. But even though I've stuck to a bland diet the past few days, the symptoms have continued.

My love to you and Eduardo,

Suzanne

From: Mark
To: Patrick

Hi Patrick,

Sorry I missed your call. Suzanne, Jennifer and I were out all day wandering around a couple of nearby towns. The best part was just watching the way the two of them enjoy each other's company. Suzanne told me Jennifer got kicked out of school last year for - get this - posting naked pictures of herself on Facebook, so I was expecting her to be a real handful but she's actually very sweet. I imagine the poor girl was just acting out after losing her father.

She simply adores Suzanne, not that I can blame her. She's a remarkable woman. We have only been seeing each other for three and a half weeks - actually 25 days but who's counting - but I feel like I've known her my entire life. We communicate with a shorthand I never had with Keiko. We're already finishing each other's sentences.

I'm going on a camping trip for a couple of days with some buddies from college. When I get back I'm going to ask Suzanne to marry me.

Yes. I know. Pre nup.

Mark

From: Catherine
To: Jean

Dear Mummy,

The love fest between Suzanne and Jennifer is as phony as a three-dollar bill, just as I suspected.

I happened to be standing outside Suzanne's door this morning and overheard the two of them arguing. I don't know what the girl wanted, but Suzanne didn't think it was a good idea. If Mark could have heard that one exchange: Suzanne's "over my dead body, you little tramp" followed by Jennifer's "step off, bitch", he wouldn't be so quick to swallow the "yes mummy" and "thanks, sweetie" crap they've been feeding him.

She's going to town tomorrow for a couple of days so at least I'll get a bit of a respite. Poor dear's got a tummy ache and has to see the doctor. She must have caught some kind of bug because she's been throwing up a lot. Here's hoping it's Ebola.

Love,

Catherine

From: Jean
To: Catherine

Get Ambler back on the case. A couple of nights in the city. With any luck the little tart won't want to spend them alone.

From: Paul
To: Suzanne

Hi Suze,

Great news! The ED is sick and I'm taking her place at the conference. I arrive in Toronto tomorrow night and will be there through Tuesday.

I know it's short notice but is there any way you can make it? I am dying to see you.

Love,

Paul

From: Suzanne
To: Paul

Hi Paul,

Fantastic news. The timing is perfect. I'm going to be in
Toronto tomorrow. I'm staying at the Hyatt. We can meet
there if you want, or I can meet you at your hotel. Whatever
works best for you.

Can't wait to see you.

Suzanne

From: Paul
To: Suzanne

I'm at the Hyatt too. They screwed up the reservation so
they're putting me up in the penthouse suite. Plenty of room
for you.

From: Suzanne
To: Paul

Penthouse suite. Two of my favorite words. See you tomorrow
night.

From: Suzanne
To: Lisa

Dear Lisa,

Paul is coming to Toronto tomorrow for the conference. His boss got sick at the last minute and is sending him. I can't believe we're finally going to see each other. Now if I could only get you up here, everything would be perfect.

Love,

Suzanne

MONDAY, AUGUST 28

Subject: Suzanne Braun
From: Ambler Detective Agency
To: Jean Rogers, Catherine Rogers

<u>Re Suzanne Braun</u>

1. Surveillance of Ms. Braun began this morning at 11:15 a.m. when she left Inglewood.

2. She drove straight to Toronto. At 1:30 p.m. she went to the offices of Dr. Joanne Morton in the Rosedale Medical Building at the corner of Sherbourne and Bloor.

3. At 2:05 p.m. she went to the Imaging and X-Ray Department in the same building for an ultra sound.

4. At 2:55 she left the Rosedale Medical Building and drove to the Hyatt Hotel.

5. At 3:25 p.m. she checked into the hotel and was observed entering the penthouse suite where she remains at this time (4:25 p.m.)

Eric Ambler
President
Ambler Detective Agency

From: Catherine
To: Jean

The penthouse suite sounds promising.

From: Jean
To: Ambler Detective Agency, Catherine

Get her medical records.

From: Catherine
To: Jean

Why the medical records?

From: Jean
To: Catherine

It occurs to me that the vomiting could be morning sickness. If we're lucky, she's carrying Gary's child.

From: Lisa
To: Suzanne

What did the doctor say? Have you met Paul yet? Make sure to give him my love.

From: Suzanne
To: Lisa

Paul's due any minute. I'm at the hotel waiting for him. I'm so excited. I feel like a schoolgirl.

The doctor ordered an ultrasound. I should have the results in a couple of days.

TUESDAY, AUGUST 29

From: Suzanne
To: Lisa

Dear Lisa,

Paul just left to go to the conference. He sends you his love. I can't tell you how wonderful it was to see him again. We stayed up the whole night. Neither of us wanted to waste a second of our time together.

He told me that he's reconsidering taking the job in New York. He admitted that after eight years in Darfur, he's finally feeling burned out. That might change when he gets back there, so I'm not counting on it, but I can't help letting my imagination run away with itself.

I have to meet my lawyer about the sale of the house, and then I'm meeting someone from the auction house to discuss selling the contents. After that my body, heart and soul will turn to Inglewood.

Love,

Suzanne

Subject: Suzanne Braun
From: Ambler Detective Agency
To: Jean Rogers, Catherine Rogers

Re: Suzanne Braun

1. At 6:50 p.m. last night, Ms. Braun met a man in the hotel lobby of the Hyatt Hotel. The man was later identified as Mr. Paul Brown, in whose name the penthouse suite was registered.

2. The two ate dinner in the hotel restaurant and then returned to the penthouse suite where they spent the night.

3. At 1:45 a.m. they ordered oysters and a bottle of champagne from room service.

4. At 8:45 a.m. this morning, they had breakfast in the hotel restaurant. Mr. Brown then attended a conference on International Refugees that is taking place at the hotel.

5. Ms. Braun left the hotel at that time and drove to the law offices of Cox and Weiner.

Yours truly,

Eric Ambler
President
Ambler Detective Agency

From: Jean
To: Catherine

Dear Catherine,

I hate for you to have to be the one to tell Mark about this, but he needs to see Ambler's report as soon as possible.

It breaks my heart to know how much this is going to hurt him, but if he'd had the good sense to listen to us in the first place, he wouldn't be in this position. At least we will finally be rid of this horrible woman.

Daddy and I arrive Thursday afternoon and we'll drive straight to Inglewood from the airport.

Love,

Mummy

From: Catherine
To: Maggie

Hi Mags,

I showed the detective's report to Mark as soon as he got back from his camping trip. He read it without saying a word, looked through me like I didn't exist, and then went to his room and packed his bags. There goes the family reunion. Oh well. It's a small price to pay if it means the end of Suzanne. Which I think it does. Literally. Mark is outside right now, waiting for Suzanne to arrive, and pacing around in a homicidal rage. Any ideas on how to get rid of a body?

I can't wait to see the look on her face when he confronts her with the report. Is that petty of me? Do I care?

love,

Catherine

WEDNESDAY, AUGUST 30

From: Mark
To: Jean

What gave you the right to hire a private detective to snoop into Suzanne's affairs just because she doesn't fit your vision of a proper daughter-in-law? I don't know if one is legally allowed to divorce your family, but consider us divorced. I don't want anything more to do with any of you. As far as I'm concerned you don't exist. Don't bother trying to contact me. I will not answer your phone calls or your emails and I will throw your letters into the trash where they belong.

From: Suzanne
To: Lisa

Dear Lisa,

I have left Inglewood for good.

I arrived yesterday evening, eager for my lover's warm embrace. Mark was waiting for me outside the cottage but if he wished to take me in his arms, it was only to wring my neck. He advanced towards me, and in terms too graphic to repeat, accused me of being unfaithful. He then presented me with a detective's report of my visit with Paul that purported to substantiate the loathsome charge. I read through it and then returned it with a shrug. "Don't bother trying to deny it," he fiercely cautioned. "I won't," I said. "Every word is true." "Do you have anything to say for yourself?" he sputtered. "Do you not have any shame?"

I asked him if he was accusing me of incest. The question stopped him in his tracks. When I explained that our brother had changed his name to Brown, his rage soon yielded to remorse. He apologized, in the most abject manner, for his unpardonable mistrust. He said he should have known that I would never betray him, and begged for my forgiveness. I could not stand to see him suffer, and told him that the matter was forgotten. If I had been in his place, I said, I would have felt the same. He thanked me for my understanding, but said he knew that wasn't true. I was too fine a person to, as he had done, assume the worst. Proof indeed, if proof be needed, that love is blind

I told him that I would understand if he wished to stay at Inglewood to see his parents who arrive tomorrow, but Jennifer and I would remain for no longer than was necessary to collect our belongings. He said he would leave with us but first he had some final words for Catherine that I would surely want to hear.

My heart surged with pride as he told her of his love for me. He then returned the detective's report to her and suggested, most impracticably, where it might best be stored. I did not have a camera to record the moment, but the final image of Catherine

- collapsed on the couch, legs splayed, eyes glazed, cheeks hollowed, mouth ajar - will forever remain imprinted on my memory.

We are now comfortably ensconced in a suite at the Shangri-La where we will remain until Mark is able to find us more permanent accommodations.

Jennifer's friend Zoe is flying to Geneva tomorrow, and as Jennifer is keen to get acclimatized to her new surroundings, we have agreed that it makes sense for her to accompany her. Although she is eager to begin this exciting new chapter in her life, I was happy to see that the little girl who needs her mother has not entirely disappeared. As we were packing her bags, she made me promise to write her every month, but thoughtfully went on to say that if that was too onerous a task, I could simply give her a series of post-dated checks.

Love,

Suzanne

THURSDAY, AUGUST 31

From: Mark
To: Jeff

I fedexed the proposal to you this morning so you should have it in a couple of days.

Looks like the trip is going to turn into a honeymoon. I proposed to Suzanne today. She wants to discuss it with her daughter before she accepts but that has more to do with her sensitivity for Jennifer's feelings than any concern that she'll object. She just doesn't want to present the girl with a fait accompli. That's the kind of woman she is.

From: Jeff
To: Mark

Congratulations! I told Marilyn and she is as thrilled as I am. She's dying to meet Suzanne so she's decided to come to Paris too.

I'll get back to you as soon as I've read the proposal.

From: Lisa
To: Suzanne

Dearest Suzanne,

Your news brightened my day and I hope that the course of true love will now run smooth.

My Schatzie has given me a most memorable 25th wedding anniversary present: a one-week safari to Brazil. We leave tomorrow.

I intend to shoot nothing but photographs but Eduardo is convinced he was a big game hunter in a previous life, and is obsessed with the idea of once again experiencing the excitement of the kill. I am appalled at the very thought but he assures me that the hunt is rigorously monitored by the conservation authorities who approve only what is necessary to preserve the balance of nature. He has already marked the spot on the wall in the lobby where he intends to mount his trophy.

Of course I will not allow this to happen, but as Schatzie's vision is suspect and he has never before fired a gun, at least not in his present incarnation, there is no need to tell him so.

Love,

Lisa

From: Suzanne
To: Lisa

Dear Lisa,

Does the course of true love ever run smooth? When I awoke this morning, Mark handed me a diamond ring no queen would find too small. On bended knee he declared his love for me, and asked me to do him the honor of becoming his wife.

I was stricken by a conscience I did not know I had. I have misled this kind and decent man into thinking that I wish to be the mother of his child and I could not bring myself to utter the words that would perpetuate this lie. Nor could I find the strength to tell the truth.

In a bid to buy myself some time, I told him that as Jennifer had so recently lost her father, I wished to discuss the matter with her before giving him my answer. His response to my prevarication only added to my shame; my "consideration" for my daughter has enhanced his good opinion of me.

I have decided to tell Mark that I cannot provide him with a child. I cannot say that his desire to have me for a wife will outweigh his yearning to become a father but be that as it may, I will not marry him under false pretenses. I told him I will give him my answer tomorrow. I pray tonight will not be our last.

Love,

Suzanne

From: Lisa
To: Suzanne

Dear Suzanne,

I am so proud of you. If there is any justice in the world, your courage will be rewarded. I won't have Internet access while we're away but I will get in touch as soon as I'm back.

Love,

Lisa

Subject: Suzanne Braun
From: Ambler Detective Agency
To: Jean Rogers, Catherine Rogers

Please find below Ms. Braun's ultra sound report.
I have confirmed that Paul Brown is the subject's brother. He changed his name from Braun on November 11, 1990.

If I can be of any further assistance, please don't hesitate to contact me.

Yours truly,

Eric Ambler
President
Ambler Detective Agency

ALLIED HEALTH NETWORK

Patient: Braun, Suzanne
Sex: F. Health #: 8835851
Client: Dr. Joanne Morton
Rosedale Medical Centre
600 Bloor St. East, Ste. 245
TORONTO, ONTARIO M6R 3N8

TEST: ABDOMINAL AND PELVIC ULTRASOUND:
Clinical History: RUQ pain, query cholecystitis

ULTRASOUND REPORT:

There are several gallstones in the gall bladder…the gall bladder
is mildly inflamed….there are no stones in the common bile
duct, and the bile ducts are of normal caliber….the liver spleen
pancreas kidneys and ovaries are all normal…. the uterus is not
seen … the rest of the exam was normal

From: Jean
To: Catherine

Darling,

I assume you've read the medical report. Daddy and I are upset
at how Mark will take the news, but we are overjoyed that we
will finally be rid of that woman.

Mummy

From: Catherine
To: Jean

What are you talking about? Suzanne's giving birth to gallstones, not to Gary's baby.

From: Jean
To: Catherine

Take a closer look at the report.

FRIDAY, SEPTEMBER 1

From: Maggie
To: Catherine

Did you have your tete-a-tete with Suzanne?

From: Catherine
To: Maggie

Hi Maggie,

Yes, and I must say I haven't had this much fun in years.

I waited until Mark left the hotel this morning before going up to their suite so that Suzanne and I could speak in private. I told her that my parents and I were very upset by the rift with Mark, that we were desperate to repair it, and that we would do anything we could to work things out. Suzanne was extremely gracious, and said she would like nothing better than to let bygones be bygones.

I admitted that I had been skeptical about her motives towards Mark, but the fact that she was willing to give him a child had convinced me that her feelings for him were genuine. She thanked me for my kind words but cautioned that at her age there was no guarantee she would be able to conceive. I told her there was no need to worry about that, reproductive technology was so advanced that any woman could have a baby provided of course, I joked, that she still had a uterus.

That's when I handed her the report.

She turned an interesting shade of white. I remember thinking it would be perfect for the guest room. I told her not to despair, she could always tell Mark she'd forgotten about her hysterectomy. Then she said she didn't expect me to believe her, but she was planning to tell Mark herself. I told her she was right, I didn't believe her, which is why I had left a copy of the report for him at the front desk.

Let's celebrate. Dinner at North 44. On me.

Love,

Catherine

From: Suzanne
To: Lisa

Dear Lisa,

You've probably already left on your safari so I suppose you won't see this for a week.

My worst fears have been realized. When I awoke this morning Mark had already departed for his morning run, leaving behind three dozen red roses and a note reiterating his love for me. It broke my heart to read it, but it did not lessen my resolve to confess to my deceit as soon as he returned.

It was then that Catherine arrived, and I learned that my fate was already sealed. She had obtained medical records proving I could not have a child and, eager to apprise Mark of the fact, had left a copy for him with the concierge.

When Mark returned, report in hand, he demanded to know why I had deceived him. I told him of my recent change of heart, but even to my ears it sounded like a child's fabrication, and he treated it as such. Did I expect him to believe it was a coincidence that I acquired scruples at the very moment my lie was to be revealed? I asked him if it really mattered. Would he not admit that even if he had heard the truth from me, it would have driven him from my side? If I could not provide him with an heir, he had no use for me. Was that not the truth? What he said next nearly broke my heart in two. He said he would admit to no such thing, and asked if I had I ever heard him say that he must be the biological father of his child?

I begged him to give our love a second chance. He responded to my plea with a bitter laugh. He could not trust me, he said, and without trust there could be no love. He then departed and demanded I be gone when he returned.

I packed my bags and then called Jennifer and told her that she would have to return to Canada. Her reaction - a series of inventive curses that would do a sailor proud - was a warning that the days ahead will be full of struggle. How I cope will tell me much about myself.

I am determined not to dwell on my misfortune. Aside from you and Paul, only Mark and Jennifer have a hold on my affections, and I have wronged them both. With Mark, there is nothing I can do to set things right. With Jennifer, there may yet be time to make amends.

Love,

Suzanne

FRIDAY, SEPTEMBER 8

From: Mark
To: Jeff

Hi Jeff,

The changes you made to the proposal are fine. I'll get you the revised version in a day or two. Look forward to seeing you and Marilyn on the 16th.

Mark

From: Jeff
To: Mark

Sounds good. I bumped into Keiko yesterday. She said she's expecting in December. Didn't you guys split up in May? I'm no mathematician but …

Jeff

From: Mark
To: Jeff

It can't be mine, we stopped having sex in January. First Suzanne, now this. I'm thinking of changing my name to Patsy.

From: Maggie
To: Catherine

Hi Cat,

No flies on your brother. Monique saw him Friday at the Quail and Firkin downing shooters with a gorgeous blonde and David saw him last night at Canoe having dinner with a cute redhead. I guess everybody grieves in his own way.

love,

Maggie

From: Catherine
To: Maggie

Hi Mags,

Why do men feel that making a conquest is the only way they can regain their self-esteem? Underneath all that bluster, they're really quite pathetic, aren't they? Still, I shouldn't be too hard on Mark. After a praying mantis, a bimbo is a step in the right direction.

He hasn't talked to us since it happened. Mummy's distraught, of course. I keep telling her that he'll come around eventually, but it's in one ear and out the other. All she can talk about is how much she misses her 'baby.'

Love,

Catherine

From: Lisa
To: Suzanne

Dear Suzanne,

We just returned to civilization so I have only now seen your email. How are you and Jennifer doing?

Eduardo and I enjoyed the safari. Unfortunately Schatzie is not cut out to be a big game hunter. He did not fire his rifle once despite being presented with several opportunities, and he wept copiously on the two occasions when our companions managed to make a kill.

Love,

Lisa

From: Suzanne
To: Lisa

Dear Lisa,

Much has happened since you left. Jennifer and I are living in a small flat on the third floor of a house in High Park - I decided to relocate in an area where I would be unlikely to encounter reminders of my former life - and I have been able to find employment as a saleswoman at a nearby clothing store. The salary is laughable but it is sufficient to put food on the table and a roof over our heads. The most important thing is that the hours are regular which will allow me to give Jennifer the stable environment she so desperately needs.

I knew it was not going to be easy for her to adjust to our new reality - her life has been turned upside down no less than my own - but I had no idea it was going to be this difficult. Her attitude towards me is more disrespectful than ever.

Yesterday I finally forced her to sit down and talk. I told her I was sorry that things had not worked out as we had hoped, but that we had no choice but to accept the situation. I said I knew how unhappy she was, and that although I would help her in any way I could, in the final analysis she was responsible, as we all are, for her own happiness. She admitted that she had never been so miserable, and asked if I was sincere in offering my help. I was touched that she was reaching out to me, and told her that if it was within my power to grant her request, I would gladly do so. She assured me that it was. All I had to do was disappear from her life forever, or as she put it, "f--k off and die."

Despite the rocky start, I have not abandoned the hope that we will one day enjoy the loving mother-daughter relationship that is my heart's desire. I know I have failed her. I have done many things that I now regret, but none which brings me greater shame. I cannot turn back the clock. All I can do is give Jennifer the love and understanding I denied her all these years, and that I am resolved to do for so long as it takes to earn her trust.

The preoccupations of my daily life have left me little time to dwell upon the past, although I am unable to banish it entirely from my mind. I could not have imagined that I would ever miss anyone the way I miss Mark. My heart aches whenever I think of him but I know I have no one to blame but myself. Although the price I paid was heavy, I have learned my lesson. I hope that fortune will smile on me once again, and if she does, I will not let her slip away again.

Love,

Suzanne

From: Lisa
To: Suzanne

I'm very sorry to hear that things are so difficult with Jennifer. Perhaps a change of scenery would be in order. Have you spoken to Jennifer about coming to Casa Blanca?

From: Suzanne
To: Lisa

Dear Lisa,

I am still keen on the prospect of a fresh start but Jennifer does not share my enthusiasm. When I raised the subject she responded by cutting her passport into tiny pieces, and there is no point in revisiting it until the new one arrives.

Love,

Suzanne

MONDAY, SEPTEMBER 11

From: Suzanne
To: Lisa

Dear Lisa,

Terrible news. Jennifer has run away from home. She has been gone for nearly two days and I am frantic with worry.

I have only myself to blame. Friday night I sat her down and told her that if she wanted to live with me, she would have to follow a few ground rules. Rule number one was a midnight curfew. Before I could get to rule number two, she left the flat and did not return until noon the following day. I told her that if she did it again, I wouldn't let her back in. She turned around, told me to "take a good look at my ass cause you're never going to see it again" and left without a backwards glance. I felt a surge of admiration for her spirit; it did not cross my mind that she would carry out her threat.

I am at my wit's end. I spend half my time at home wondering if I should be out looking for her, and the other half driving around the city looking for her and wondering if I should be at home in case she shows up.

Suzanne

From: Patrick
To: Mark

Haven't heard from you in a while. Hope you're well. How's Ashley? Or is it Nicole? I can't keep up any more.

From: Mark
To: Patrick

Hey,

I'm good. It took me a while but after some serious soul-searching I realized that chasing after everything in a skirt wasn't making me happy. For one thing it's impossible to remember who's who and that can be pretty embarrassing. So I've decided to only go out with girls named Brittany. They're all in their twenties but I've decided not to hold that against them.

Mark

From: Patrick
To: Mark

Have you had any contact with Suzanne?

From: Mark
To: Patrick

Who?

From: Patrick
To: Mark

Tell me you are 100% positive she wasn't going to tell you she couldn't have children and I will never mention her name again.

From: Suzanne
To: Lisa

Dear Lisa,

My baby is safe and sound, and back at home. The police brought her back around six, tired, frightened and bedraggled, but otherwise none the worse for wear.

She was afraid to tell me what had happened and made me promise that I would let her stay no matter what. As if I would let her go! I was expecting a horror story, and a horror story is what I got, although, thanks only to the grace of God, she has emerged unscathed.

Her first night away from home she was 'befriended' by a young man who offered her a place to stay. She was reluctant to go with him but he promised she could have her own room with a door she could lock. The next day he told her she owed him $500 for room and board. When she said she didn't have the money, he told her she would have to prostitute herself to pay him back. When she refused, he threatened to beat her. He left, locking her into her room, and returned a few minutes later with the "john," who miraculously turned out to be an undercover policeman.

This horrible experience may yet prove to be a blessing in disguise. The tears we shed helped close the gap between us, and we both agreed to leave the past behind and start afresh. Jennifer lay in my arms until she fell asleep. I told her once again how much I loved her. I heard her tell me she loved me too, but realized I had dreamed it.

love,

Suzanne

FRIDAY, SEPTEMBER 15

From: Lisa
To: Suzanne

Dear Suzanne,

I am so excited that you and Jennifer are coming to live with us. When I spoke to her yesterday she said she was nervous about starting school in the middle of the semester. Please tell her that I spoke to the principal and he assured me that the teachers will do everything they can to make sure she catches up to the other students as quickly as possible. By the way, he was very impressed that she has been studying Spanish on her own.

Eduardo returned last night from a tour of the pampas. He is committed to introducing buffalo meat to the Argentinian diet and is certain that the pampas will prove to be ideal grazing ground. He was absolutely thrilled to hear that you and Jennifer will be joining us and spent the day cleaning the casita in preparation for your arrival.

We will pick you up at the airport tonight. I know you and Jennifer are going to love it here. Buen viaje.

Love,

Lisa

Subject: Suzanne Braun
From: Drake Mason Investigations
To: Mark Rogers

Re: Suzanne Braun

I have located Ms. Braun. She is living at 113 Evelyn Avenue. 2nd Floor. Tel: 416.555.6712

Paul Drake
President
Drake Mason Investigations

From: Patrick
To: Mark

Deborah told me you called. I'm glad to hear you've come to your senses and stuffed your foolish pride where it belongs. And yes, I'd be delighted to be your best man.

From: Suzanne
To: Lisa

Dear Lisa,

The airport limo is due to arrive in a few minutes. It has been storming here all day and my mood is as gray as the sky. The hope that Mark would come for me has occupied a secret corner of my heart but now I can no longer cling to this flimsy thread. I know that I shall never see him again.

I bear my pain without regret. Fate may have deprived me of a lover, but in so doing so she has given me a daughter, and I consider her to be on my side. In a few short weeks Jennifer has been transformed from a surly delinquent into a delightful young woman, outgoing and full of life.

She is eager to begin our new adventure, and has been practicing her Spanish on our landlady despite the fact that Teresa only speaks Portuguese and does not understand a word Jennifer is saying to her. She has also filled up most of one notebook with useful phrases, although some of them - "where did you get your nose ring?" "does this hotel have a pool bar?" and "where is the topless beach?" - give me reason to think that vestiges of her former self remain.

I want to thank you and Eduardo again for the kindness you have shown to Jennifer and I. See you tonight.

Love,

Suzanne

From: Mark
To: Patrick

Suzanne and Jennifer have left the country. Believe it or not, they are moving to Morocco.

When I got to Suzanne's house, the Portuguese landlady was there but she couldn't speak a word of English, she just kept saying 'not here, not here.' I went door to door until I found a Portuguese-speaking neighbor who could translate. She told me that Suzanne and Jennifer had gone to Casablanca.

I leave for Paris tomorrow. I'll get in touch when I'm back.

From: Suzanne
To: Lisa

Dear Lisa,

Our flight was cancelled due to bad weather. They've put us up in a hotel near the airport and we're rebooked for the same flight tomorrow.

Love,

Suzanne

hola, tia Lisa. Aqui Jennifer. nos vemos Domingo.

SATURDAY, SEPTEMBER 16

Subject: Vive la France
From: Suzanne
To: Lisa

Dear Lisa,

We arrived in Paris this evening, exhausted but far too excited to sleep.

With all that has happened in the past 12 hours, it is hard not to believe in a divine providence. How else to explain the unlikely confluence of events which has brought us here: the thunderstorm that kept us in Toronto for an extra day, the computer malfunction that had us changing gates from one end of the terminal to the other, the hair floating in my fresh-squeezed orange juice that sent me back to the cafe where I bought it, the rudeness of the clerk who would not give me a refund, my impetuous decision to throw the juice in his face, his roar of outrage that attracted the attention of the security guard, the guard's ill-considered belief that I needed to be restrained, my instinctive reaction to slap him in the face, his unnecessary call for reinforcements, the curiosity of the crowd that soon gathered around us.

Without each and every one of these events, Mark's eyes would never have strayed from his book, and like two ships passing in the night, we would now be far apart.

The cheers that erupted when he got down on his knees and asked me to marry him are still resounding in my ears.

We have decided to get married here in Paris and have set the date for this Wednesday. I know it is short notice but I hope that you and Eduardo will be able to join us. It will be a small affair. The only other guests are Mark's friends Jeff and Patrick and their wives.

Please tell me that you are coming.

Love,

Suzanne

From: Lisa
To: Suzanne

Dear Suzanne,

Eduardo and I will both come to the wedding. Neither of us will miss it for the world. It took some doing, but Eduardo was able to reschedule his meeting with the assistant to the fourth undersecretary of the Ministry of Agriculture for the end of the month.

The manner in which you and Mark found each other confirms

that you are true soul mates. I happened to mention to Eduardo that as much as I had wanted this for you, I never imagined that it would actually happen. Schatzie reminded me that his mother had predicted no less and gently chastised me for my lack of faith.

My heart is filled with joy.

Love,

Lisa

From: Suzanne
To: Catherine

Dear Catherine,

I am writing in the hope that we can put the past behind us. I know that you will think that it is easy for me to be magnanimous, now that Mark is mine.

Mark is mine, Mark is mine. How lovely those three words. But I digress. I do not expect you to shed your animosity towards me overnight. It cannot be easy to accept that your Herculean efforts to keep us apart have fallen short. Only a saint could bear no rancor at having her hopes frustrated at every turn. To believe that victory is within one's grasp only to see it slip away is a bitter pill for anyone to swallow.

I understand all that, but I also know your feelings towards me have their roots in ancient hurts and I do not think that we can move on without addressing them. I don't know if you will believe me, but when Michael first asked me out, I told him that I would not say yes as long as he was seeing you. That was my duty as your friend. When he later told me that the obstacle - his word not mine - had been removed, I was, by any moral code, free of further obligation. What point would have been served by sending him away? It would not have brought him to your side.

Believe me when I tell you I had no idea that you loved him so. It was only later, after he had declared his love for me, that he told me how your heart was broken. He told me how you threw yourself at his feet, clutched his legs, and begged him not to go; he told me of the midnight phone calls when you pleaded for a second chance, of your threats to end your life. Do you think that did not move me? To learn that one I used to call a friend had debased herself like this, to know that not a shred of dignity was left. Of course it did.

It is a relief to have unburdened myself. I hope you feel the same. It may be some time before we see each other again, and while I wait for that day to come, I remain,

Your sister-in-law,

Suzanne

SUNDAY, OCTOBER 31

From: Suzanne
To: Lisa

Dear Lisa,

We came back from Guatemala City yesterday with Sylvia. We weren't able to meet the birth mother, the agency advised against it. All we know about her is that she's a 16 year-old girl from a small village.

Sylvia is absolutely delightful, beautiful black eyes and chubby cheeks. Pictures are on the way! Mark is in seventh heaven, and so if Jennifer. We offered to send her back to Switzerland but she said she wants to stay here with us.

I have to admit I never thought I'd be a mother again, but if it has to be, this is the way to do it. No stretch marks and a live-in nanny.

Love,

Suzanne

ABOUT THE AUTHOR

MICHAEL BETCHERMAN is an award-winning screenwriter and author with numerous credits in both documentary and dramatic television. He is the author of two young-adult novels: *Breakaway,* which was shortlisted for the John Spray Mystery Award, and *Face-Off*, which was shortlisted for the Arthur Ellis Mystery Award. Both books were published by Penguin Group (Canada). He is also the author of the romantic comedy, *Suzanne,* and co-author, with David Diamond, of the mystery novel, *The Daughters of Freya.*

Readers are invited to contact the author by email at mbetcherman@gmail.com

Made in the USA
Columbia, SC
17 August 2017